All about the Staffordshire Bull Terrier

Also by John F. Gordon

All about the Boxer
All about the Cocker Spaniel

All about the Staffordshire Bull Terrier

JOHN F. GORDON

PELHAM BOOKS

First published in Great Britain by
PELHAM BOOKS LTD
44 Bedford Square
London, WC1B 3DU
1984

British Library Cataloguing in Publication Data

Gordon, John F.
  All about the Staffordshire bull terrier.
  1.Staffordshire bull terrier
  I. Title
  636.7'55   SF429.S85

ISBN 0 7207 1497 4

Filmset by Cambrian Typesetters, Aldershot, Hants
Printed and bound in Great Britain by Butler & Tanner Ltd,
Frome and London

Contents

List of Illustrations

Photographs

Line drawings

Photo credits

Historic Dog Features (pages 3, 5, 6, 13, 15, 17, 20 and 26); Keith Yuill
(page 40); J.K. and E.A. McFarlane (pages 52 *top* and 129); Hal (page 52
bottom); C.M. Cooke (page 58 *bottom*); Frank Garwood (pages 63
bottom, 80, 81, 103, 113 and 114); Anne Cumbers (page 74); Mansell
Balance (122).

Preface

I am indebted to the very many breed enthusiasts whose appreciation of my *The Staffordshire Bull Terrier Owner's Encyclopaedia* prompted them to enquire as to a revision when that title neared to the end of its successful run. The publishers, in their wisdom, have decided to include our breed in their popular 'All About . . .' series and this book is the result. Much of the Encyclopaedia has been incorporated in the volume, but I have tried to make this work as complete as the space at my disposal permits. When one prepares a monograph on a breed such as this, it is inevitably with a sense of having trodden somewhere along the line on ground which has already been adequately covered and this applies especially to matters of the breed's origin and history. Always fascinated by the blood sports into which the old type Staffordshire Bull Terrier took such an active part, I have covered this part of the breed's gladiatorial past with some fullness, for I believe that like myself, many dyed-in-the-wool fanciers enjoy entering into this past world of the breed's history; fondly imagining perhaps, that their own dogs carry still the courage and the ability to fight and combat in the pit and field arenas with the success of their early forebears.

The Staffordshire Bull Terrier is my original love in the world of dogs. No other breed can claim such a substantial worth in my thoughts. When I first entered the fancy, it was a breed not thought much of, small in its numbers and yet with owners who were the 'salt of the earth'. Today, it is one of the most popular Terriers and has quality breed members in virtually every country in the world. It is a breed worth writing about and worth avid reading for it will go to even greater heights of popularity. I hope readers will find this book an interesting one – it has most of the essential facts about the breed, put in what I hope will prove an interesting and easily understandable form.

John F. Gordon
Romford
1983

1 Origins and History

Early Progenitors

As with all modern breeds of dog, it is virtually impossible to be specific in the complex matters of origin and history. The Staffordshire Bull Terrier is no exception to this difficulty, although we are aware that he stems firmly from a rootstock steeped in antiquity which he shares with the Old English Bulldog. Unlike that classic breed however, his more recent evolutionary progress – namely that which occurred during the decades which overlapped the change from the eighteenth to the nineteenth century – remains clouded, at least to some extent.

An interesting, if assumptive, chart was formed by Edwin Megargee to show the family tree of one hundred and fourteen different breeds of dog, showing a small civet-like creature named *Tomarctus*, which lived some fifteen million years ago. This animal is believed by many cynologists to be the ancestor common to all dogs. However, with what *factual* material we are fortunate enough to possess, it would seem that the early progenitors of the Staffordshire Bull Terrier existed many centuries ago running as heavy dogs of the chase. The period under review could have been six centuries and more before the birth of Christ. The major ancestral type was clearly the Old English Mastiff (as we know it from early art). This great dog descended from the original Molossian Dog of Athens, a formidable canine, whose appearance must have petrified most of his adversaries. In the *Anecdotes of Dogs*, 1858, Jesse depicts him as 'a dog of gigantic size, of a yellowish colour with a black muzzle'; a description which fits not only the Molossus, but the ancient Mastiff. The Molossus was bred in Epirus in Ancient Greece, evidently around the area of Molossi, where an important amphitheatre for the conduct of old Roman sports was established. A plaster reproduction of this dog is to be seen in the Metropolitan Museum of Arts, New York, fashioned about 400 BC by an unknown artist. These huge Grecian Mastiffs were used for the most barbarous of arena sports and it is reported that they committed themselves with great savagery and skill.

The dog was bred extensively and shipped to Rome and beyond by the Procurator Cynegii, an executive appointed by Roman Emperors to keep the amphitheatres well-stocked with warring beasts. Countries in the western world soon encountered these dogs, and once domiciled they were bred from and developed individually. Very often, according to where they were bred they developed slight alterations in type from the original parental stock. Maybe this variation would be confined to coat texture, maybe bulk of head and muzzle, more often than not to size. What seldom varied was the temperament of the dog which seemed to remain fierce, bold and tenacious. From this early Molossian, it is certain that our Old English Mastiff developed. From the Molossus, too, came similar Mastiff-type breeds in other countries: the Branchiero of Italy, Rottweiler of Southern Germany, the Dogue de Bordeaux of France, the English Bulldog, the Tibetan Mastiff, and even the St Bernard owes strong ancestral affinity to the Molossian. All these breeds were used at times for combat sports, some kinds more than others, but all were built and bred to attack Man's enemies as well as their own. The Bullenbeisser, progenitor of the Boxer developed in Germany, and most of these big guard-dog breeds owe their existence to the Mastiffs which were left by the Romans in all the many parts of Asia and Europe through which they passed.

It is thought that some big dogs were brought into England by the itinerant trading Phoenicians, long before the birth of Christ. Bands of them were said to have been used by our ancient forefathers in repelling invaders around our coasts. Even later Roman expeditionary forces were said to have been impressed by these great dogs, probably developments of their own earlier stock. They were described by Gratius Faliscus in 8 AD as the 'Pugnaces of Britain' and by the poet Claudian as the 'broad-mouthed dogs' of Britain. It is conceivable that the Romans would have returned to their homeland with examples of this British stock and used them for improving their own strains as well as testing their worth in the arenas.

This Old English Mastiff would have been the forerunner of our present-day Mastiff. From the Mastiff group would have emerged the Bond-dog or Bandogge, known also as the Englische Dogge. These dogs were smaller in girth than the Mastiff proper and were the immediate progenitors of the Bulldog and subsequently the Bull Mastiff. Such animals were large, by modern standards, although certainly much 'rangier' with great thrust and power and an aggressive, fearless nature, especially where other animals were concerned.

They sported a variety of coat colours, red, brindle, fallow and piebald, often all white and patched, markings inherited no doubt from the Alan or Alaunt an ancestor from the early fifteenth century. The Bandogge was used mainly as a chained guard dog but was brought out occasionally for bull-baiting. His name means literally, Bond-dog, i.e. a dog held in bondage or chained-up, a lifestyle which rendered him extremely fierce and intractable. He was much feared for his vicious appearance and staunch devotion to guard duties, and he received scant respect from the public, regarded by many as a brainless, savage monster. Even F. Cuvier was purported to have asserted that the Bulldog of his day had a brain smaller in proportion to any other of his cogenitors.* Such a statement is today considered so wide of the truth as to be laughable; stubborn the breed might well be, but never short of brains and acumen. Neither is there any reason to suppose that he varied from other canines four hundred and more years ago. A number of these early Bulldogs found their way to Germany, Spain and southern France where they speedily became fashionable and assumed a much smarter exterior than the resident Bull breed. From this dog's influence there arose improvements in the German Bullenbeisser of the day, forerunner of our modern Boxer, cousin of the interesting Brabanter breed. All these dogs, including the Spanish Bulldog, the Dogue de Bordeaux and other offshoots, were used for Continental bull-baiting and similar nefarious pastimes.

"Top," a pure Bulldog, the Property of C. Stockdale, Esq.

'Top', a pure Bulldog of his day (1879) owned by Stockdale, from a drawing by L. Wells.

No one had attempted any proper division of the breeds or any clarification of the various functions until the Elizabethan sage, Dr Johannes Caius (John Keyes, founder of Caius College), attempted it in 1570. This was written in Latin (see *De Canibus Britannicus*) but later

* *The Dog, In Health and Disease*, 1859 by 'Stonehenge' (J. H. Walsh).

translated by Abraham Fleming in *Of English Dogges, the Diversities, the Names, the Natures, and the Properties*, 1576. The Mastiff or Bandogge is therein described as '. . . vast, huge, stubborne, augly and eager, of a heavy and burthenous body and therefore of little swiftness, terrible and fearful to behold, and more fearse and fell than any Arcadian curre'. The word Mastiff (or Mastive or Mastyve) derives from an Anglo Saxon word 'masty' meaning fat or massive, which constitutes a fair description of the dog. In the sixteenth century dogs were usually named according to their appearance or function. The Caius table which includes the Mastiff is shown below:

Dogges comprehended in ye fourth secion are these	The Shepherds Dogge The Mastive or Bandogge	which hat sundry names derived from sundry circumstances as	The Keeper or Watchman The Butcher's Dogge The Messinger or Carrier The Mooner The Water Drawer The Tinckers Curr The Fencer

The Mastiff, it will be seen, carries a great deal of importance as an ancestor of the Staffordshire Bull Terrier, by producing the Bulldog to which in later years a Terrier was to be introduced in the desire to form a faster, more active breed of dog.

Bulldog–Terrier relationship

When dog-fighting came into its own, it was natural that efforts should be made to improve the speed and display of the sport, and the most obvious subject to receive close attention in the reform was the pit dog himself. The early fighting Bulldog, while possessing ample courage and tenacity, by virtue of his size and substance lacked great agility. In the dog pit rapidity of movement often proved the deciding factor in a fight where weight, gameness and skill might be evenly matched. Thus, it was not long before breeders turned to the serious task of producing a 'new look' dog which was fearless and tenacious, yet faster in attack and battle. We know now that their efforts, although diverse in many respects, met with a strong measure of success, for this ideal was eventually produced in the dog we know as the Staffordshire Bull Terrier. It was at this stage that a certain amount of confusion exists as to the exact methods used in producing the Staffordshire. There are two

'Terriers', from an engraving by J. Clarke after Henry Alken. This shows a group of early 19th century Terriers of the types probably used to cross with the Old English Bulldog to create the 'Bull-and-Terrier'.

theories advanced and either or both may be true, for they are allied in certain respects. Even in present-day discussion circles each theory has its ardent supporters. The theories are:

1. That the Staffordshire Bull Terrier is actually a direct and virtually unadulterated descendant of the original Bulldog of about 1800, bred on lighter and more Terrier-like lines, with no or very few Terrier crossings.
2. That the Staffordshire Bull Terrier's principal ancestors were the Old English Bulldog of about 1800 and a small, smooth-coated game Terrier, probably the Old English Terrier, now extinct.

As the Author has indicated in his monograph *The Staffordshire Bull Terrier Handbook*, 1951, some support may be given to the first theory by a study of old paintings and prints showing the typical Bulldog of the period. Abraham Cooper's famous oil painting of 1816 'Crib' and 'Rosa', shows 'Rosa' (stated to be representative of the finest Bulldog blood of her day) as a bitch with the body, loins, legs, feet, tail and quarters of a reasonably typical Staffordshire Bull Terrier. This is offset somewhat by her tendency to 'layback' in muzzle, but such muzzle formations are notorious for their inability to cement in breeding and the lengthening of natural foreface would be comparatively easy in the hands of an experienced breeder. Other portraits by contemporary artists show

'Rosa'. One of the old Bull-and-Terriers, owned by the Baroness Burdett-Coutts, from a painting by G. Morley (1891).

similar characteristics, and it seems clear, therefore, that the modern Bulldog resembles his original ancestors less than the Staffordshire Bull Terrier resembles the old Bulldogs, giving some credence to the suggestion that the Staffordshire Bull Terrier is actually the old Bulldog bred on more Terrier-like lines. The modern Bulldog, as we know it, was evolved by the efforts of sportsmen of that period who preferred a dog lower to ground, wider-fronted, generally cloddier, with exaggerated layback and lighter quarters, than did their contemporaries.

A written picture of the Bulldog of 1855–60 is given by James Watson in his *The Dog Book*, 1906: 'The Bulldog of this period was totally unlike the dog of today. He was only moderately low on the leg and stood closer in front than our exaggerations do. His tail, more frequently than not was a plain whip tail, and he lacked the massiveness in head of the later day dog.' It should be remembered that this description fitted the dog well over a quarter of a century after the period we have discussed, and shows even at that time little progress had been made towards the finished product. Twenty years later however, breeders were very much nearer the type of Bulldog we now accept, as can be seen by the coloured plates of 'Smasher' and 'Doon Brae' in Vero Shaw's *Illustrated Book of the Dog*, 1879–81, and reproduced in Clifford Hubbard's *Literature of British Dogs* (pl.XI), 1949.

Personally, while not entirely accepting this theory, it is one which appeals quite strongly, for it suggests that the Staffordshire has descended from purer blood lines than divers crossings would have allowed. However, what cannot be ignored are the pronounced Terrier characteristics, both in physical make-up and temperament which appear in most modern Staffordshire Bull Terriers. These, coupled with the suggestive names 'Bulldog-Terrier' and 'Bull-and-Terrier' handed down to us by nineteenth-century writers on the breed, make it reasonably certain that Terrier blood was mixed with that of the Old English Bulldog, so that a smaller and more active dog might be made. This brings us to the second and more acceptable theory.

It seems reasonably certain that, from the facts available, i.e. those gleaned from early writers, that the first crossings were made soon after 1800, the original Bulldog being crossed with a small, smooth coated Terrier of some 9kg (20lb) in weight. There is no reference to the issue at the time apart from calling them Terriers. However, Pierce Egan in his *Annals of Sporting*, 1822 (Vol.I) used for the first time, we believe, the name 'Bull Terrier'. Captain Thomas Brown gave the breed a paragraph under the same name in his book *Biographical Sketches and Authentic Anecdotes of Dogs*, 1829. The breed responsible for the Terrier side was almost certainly the Old English Terrier, a breed of dubious type which appeared in both smooth and rough coats, the former kind being the sort used in the early matings. Black-and-tan coloration was not uncommon to this dog, but the coat types were so varied that we learn from early show catalogues and from writers on the breed that it was a dog not able to reproduce its own kind with any degree of certainty, hence its early extinction.

Thus, by using this small, 9kg (20lb) variety of Terrier with the somewhat rangy, perhaps Terrier-like, Bulldog of the day, a dog of around 27kg (60lb) stock was produced, but which could vary in weight on maturity to between 9kg (20lb), and 27kg (60lb) in extreme cases, according to the parental background. These Bull-and-Terriers or Bulldog-Terriers were the ancestors of our Staffordshire Bull Terrier. The newcomers appeared in all the colours common to the Bulldog: reds, fawns, fallows, brindles of all shades and very often black-and-tans. Most of these colours would be mixed with white and all were acceptable; for no good fighting dog was a bad colour according to the tenets of the sportsmen of that time. However, in a later century black-and-tans were to be ostracized by the men who pioneered the Staffordshire Bull Terrier to the show bench.

Of course, Terrier breeds other than the Old English Terrier would

'Young Storm' and 'Old Storm', the Paddington Bulldogs of about 1820. These weighed about 70lbs each.

have been used; in fact, one can assume freely, I think, that any sporting little Terrier with a smooth coat would have been considered a likely candidate for these unions. Early pictures of Terriers show some with a distinct leanness in the head with some snipiness, which has in the past been noted in some Staffords, but we hope this is being bred out for seldom today is a bad example of this fault seen.

Let us accept then that the Staffordshire Bull Terrier is the scion of the Bulldog and the Terrier. This proved a factual breeding formula, aided by prudent selection and development. Nevertheless, type or stamp of issue was not the main requirement of the old breeders. They wanted gameness and bold heart first, good looks being secondary. They bred their dogs to bitches who had won pit battles and frankly, as far as they were concerned, it did not matter too much what the bitch looked like. Gradually, as the twentieth century approached, their outlooks changed a little. They realised that the best battlers had to have the best ammunition. Dogs needed big biting heads and jaws, and they also required big muscled legs to thrust themselves into an adversary, strong necks, big ribs, short backs and deep chests. With such they lasted longer in battle and won their fights over less physically endowed specimens. Such necessities encouraged them to start breeding for these points; as any dog breeder who knows his subject is aware, by careful selection and studious application over a comparatively short period, one can produce almost any desired shape, colour, type, size or variety of dog.

To complete a proper picture, one must also breed for a desired temperament, but to maintain the temperament of any breed is not easy. Most varieties were bred and developed for a specific purpose. The dog who fights must be endowed not only with a will to fight but the courage to see the battle home and won to the bitter end. Our modern Stafford is produced largely with beauty for show in mind, but he must have a true breed temperament nevertheless; without that he is no Staffordshire Bull Terrier in the true meaning of the breed as one wants him to inherit the temperament of his forefathers. This is not an easy wish to realise, for today one cannot introduce a dog to bull-baiting sessions on Sunday mornings and Bank Holidays, neither can we trek to some sordid dog-fighting meet to test the merits of our favourite. Dog-fighting, once so very popular, now justly with a veil drawn over it as a degrading sport, might have kept Stafford spirit and fire at a high order. The fact of the matter is that today we have no true test of courage for our dog. If we have a bitch, we can never be sure that the dog we use with her carries the right sort of bold heart in his body. It is temperament that matters immensely. Successful bull-baiting dogs were bred in the early days to bitches proven thrice and more in the affray, and no doubt about it, such dams threw the right sort of stock for which the old-time sportsman-breeder got good financial return. The best we can do in modern times is to be cautious; make sure the dog we use is a good upstanding stallion at least in character and courage. Ensure too that the dam, who has produced the puppy you might buy, is no shirker when it comes to action. Being selective in such matters is your contribution to Stafford-shire Bull Terrier future. Remember in showing, that a vicious, screaming Staffordshire is seldom, if ever, a typical one; although a dog in the ring being judged with others can be excused some aggressiveness. It can be expected of some perhaps lesser breeds to display nervous venom in their make-up; such dogs are seldom called upon to prove their intentions, but a Stafford might be and it is a disgrace to his breed and strain if he fails his test. Remember that, if true Stafford temperament is allowed to dilute and finally die out, the breed's popularity will wane irretrievably and eventually die with it.

Appearance in art and literature

Dogs similar in appearance to the Pugnaces of Britain described earlier are shown in many Greek, Egyptian and Roman friezes. Particularly striking resemblances may be seen in Assyrian bas-reliefs executed about

600 BC, even earlier. These antiquities and the later appearance of the Staffordshire Bull Terrier's forebears in art, verse and prose will ever prove a vast source of interest and fascination for the students of our breed. Comparatively modern renderings will include the outstanding reproductions of Mastiffs shown in the paintings 'Venus and Adonis' by Titian (c.1487–1576), and 'The Children of Charles I' by Van Dyck (1599–1641), the latter work showing an immense dog which completely dwarfs the subjects of the painting. J. E. Ridinger, the German painter and engraver (1698–1767) was responsible for some wonderful informative work on large Bull-type dogs showing them in sport and repose. George Morland, the English painter (1763–1804), is of particular interest to us, for many of his subjects were of the bull-breed fraternity just as the breed was beginning to take shape and enter the nineteenth century. The engraving by James Linnell of Morland's 'The Turnpike Gate', published in 1806 shows what seems to be a particularly good specimen of the era. The same artist's 'The Country Butcher', engraved by J. R. Smith, published 1802 depicts a typical 'Butcher's Dog' easily visualised in the thick of a bull-bait melée.

It is however, in the time of Elizabeth I and following upon her reign that we are able to learn much of the early Mastiff and Bulldog. In those days, the interest in what we term blood sports was at its height. The old Bear Garden in Southwark was a popular rendezvous for Londoners of all denominations and it is natural that these pastimes received the attentions of contemporary artists. From them we learn a great deal of the more common forms of vulgar sport such as bull-, bear- and badger-baiting coupled with other diversions.

Nineteenth-century artists, such as Clark, the Alkens and Cruikshank, depict these sports with consummate skill, although some excellent work is recorded anonymously. Paintings of the period showing the forebears of our Staffordshire are in the main, privately owned, many having gone to America. Possibly one of the most famous 'old ones' is that of 'Crib and Rosa' by Abraham Cooper, R.A. (c.1816) and this shows perfect examples of the early Bulldog form, referred to earlier. Another famous painting is that of H. B. Chalon's 'Wasp, Child and Billy', three very likely ancestors of the Staffordshire Bull Terrier, which was published on 15th May, 1809. The picture was later engraved by William Ward, who held the title of Engraver Extraordinary to HRH the Prince of Wales and Duke of York. His work was published by Randon and Sneath's Sporting Gallery in Bloomsbury Square. A legend to the engraving reads: 'The above Bulldogs (the property of Henry Boynton, Esq.) originally of the late Duke of Hamilton's breed and the only left of that blood, are in such estimation that Mr B. has refused 120 guineas for Billy and 20 guineas for a whelp before taken from the bitch. It is asserted that they are the only real Bull in existence and that upon their decease that species of dogs may be considered as extinct.'

In literature, there is, of course, little to peruse dealing specifically with the Staffordshire Bull Terrier. Many of the old dog writers could skim near to a dog of his type only by his progenitors. There is much to read of the Mastiff and his kin, also the Bulldog with his Continental cousins. A good deal of this is bound up with divers kinds of bull-baiting and combat dogs, from which we are perforce to sort out the types which are acceptable to us as forerunners of the Stafford. The student is advised to consider these early aspects of the Staffordshire Bull Terrier, in spite of the fact that type and outline today varies so much with the ancestral stock. In the study of breed evolution one needs to develop an eye for the unfolding of canine form from its early stages to its modern stock form. The expert may well be allowed to employ his imagination in lively form at this task, for without this no true picture of a breed's progress throughout the centuries could ever be formed.

2 The Baiting Sports

Bull-baiting and bear-baiting, and the baiting of badgers, were old English pastimes. They date from the twelfth century at least, and possibly in the case of the foremost sport from the days of William the Conqueror. Any big, strong animal was fair game for the pleasure-loving Briton with his ponderous fierce dog. The Elizabethan era in particular saw these sports at the height of their popularity, using dogs possibly rather larger than the twentieth century Staffordshire Bull Terrier. These were fierce, tenacious dogs whose gameness was a byword. Actually, it is thought that bull-baiting was introduced by the then Earl Warren, Lord of Stamford, in 1209, who encouraged local butchers to put up a bull for baiting in the November of every year.

Bull-baiting

This sport soon took on throughout the country and it was not long before every market town had its bull ring or place where the bull was tethered and baited by dogs. By the end of the thirteenth century, it was Britain's leading sport and spread quickly to the Continent where dogs of a rather larger category known as Bullenbeissen were used. These dogs had developed from the early Mastiffs and all had come from the family of dogs from which Staffordshires ultimately developed. For a number of centuries the sport persisted with the use of these powerfully built dogs. Royal patronage was given to it between the latter half of the sixteenth century and the first half of the seventeenth century. It soon became the fashionable pursuit of the aristocracy who did much to encourage and promote it.

In baiting the bull, the dog was expected to pin the animal's nose to the ground and not loosen his grip. To avoid his adversary's horns, the cunning Bulldog would often approach the bull by slithering along the ground on his belly. Consequently, as a small dog was far less likely to encounter the big beast's horns than a larger dog, a smaller, low-slung Bulldog came into being. This kind soon gained enormous popularity and it was from this tighter, compact form that the modern Staffordshire Bull Terrier took much of his make-up and shape. The bull himself became quite adept in the craft of battle. To protect his nose from the dog he would dig out a hole with one of his forefeet so that he could sink this tender part out of the way of the dog's grasp. Frightful atrocities were perpetrated by dog owners who wished to prove the gameness of their dogs to onlookers. It is on record that one man deliberately hacked off his dog's feet, one by one, while the animal still held the bull by the nose, never once releasing his hold. This was said by his owner to confirm the dog's great tenacity!

Under James I, the sport was forbidden on Sundays, it becoming illegal with the formation of the Commonwealth. With the coming of the Restoration however, the sport was revived and it became customary for 'Masters of Publick Houses to keep or procure Bulls to baiten on certaine Holidays, so call'd, as well as other days, on purpose to draw Company to their houses'.

'Bull Broke Loose', believed to be at Barnet Fair about 1820.

It was common to tip the tines or horns of the bull with metal buttons, rather similar to the manner in which fencing foils are blunted. Bulls which were kept for repeated baiting had this done to them. It prevented the attacking dog from being gored, for the 'sport' was to toss the dog, not to gore it. Occasionally, a bull tormented beyond endurance would break his tether and then pandemonium would reign, many serious casualties being caused in the crowd. At such a time, the call 'A lane! A lane!' would go out for the cowardly spectators to make a path for the infuriated bull to pass through. People would be gored or trampled to death, dogs disembowelled and other horrors and incidents would occur.

The local records of the towns in South Staffordshire give a number of illustrations of the pastime. Hackwood in his *Old English Sports*, London, 1907, gives the following announcement:

NOTICE!

'On Monday next there will be a bull baited at the Bull Ring in Sedgeley when a £5 wager will be laid on Mr. Wilke's dog Teazer of Wednesbury that he pins the bull's nose within an hour. Entries of dogs can be made at Mr. Perry's on or before Saturday. Fee, 5s.'

We learn that the dog Teazer won the wager for his backers, holding on to the bull which eventually broke loose, running as far back as Coseley. Release from the dog was obtained only when the bull's nostrils gave way, the dog falling off and being trampled to death by the bull's hooves. The poor bull was then turned back by the yelling mob, sinking exhausted on the steps of Sedgeley church when it was cudgelled to death by its pursuers.

A Parliamentary Bill in 1802, known as Martin's Act, calling for the abolition of the sport was defeated by a majority of thirteen through the eloquence of one, William Windham, who spoke in favour of bull- and bear-baiting on 24th May, 1802. However, prohibition came finally with the Humane Act of 1835, the body we know now as the Royal Society for the Prevention of Cruelty to Animals being instrumental in effecting this reform by bringing a successful test case in Lincoln Court. In spite of this edict, bull-baiting continued in hole-and-corner places throughout Britain for a few more decades, eventually to die out in favour of dog-fighting and cock-fighting, sports which could be more easily controlled and 'wrapped-up' in the event of police intervention.

The 1835 Act marks an important milestone in the history of humane progress, the credit for securing its passage going to Mr Pease, a member of the Society of Friends, who steered its course through Parliament, Mr J. G. Meymott, honorary solicitor to the SPCA (now the RSPCA) and Mr W. A. Mackinnon MP. It is the first Act which specifically mentions the dog and abolishes baiting sports:

That any person keeping, or using, any House, Room, Pit, Ground, or other place, for running, baiting or fighting any Bull, Bear, Badger, Dog, or other Animal (whether of a domestic or wild nature or kind), or for Cock-fighting, shall be liable to a penalty of £5 for every day he shall keep or use same.

This Act wholly repealed the earlier Martin's Act, but it gave the power of summary arrest, which that Act lacked.

Bear-baiting

This sport was a very simple one as far as its procedure was concerned. The bear was chained to a stake or a ring set in the wall by one hind leg or by the neck and was then worried by dogs. The pastime seems to have commenced about the time of King Henry II, and to have been abolished by the 1835 Act of Parliament already referred to.

Erasmus, writing from the house of Sir Thomas More at the beginning of the sixteenth century, records that many herds of bears were maintained in England for baiting purposes. Bear-baiting was usually a Sunday sport and in London, where it seemed to be extremely popular, it was held in pits specially erected for the purpose. The most famous of these was Paris Gardens in Southwark, this district of the Metropolis abounding in pits, large and small, catering for blood sports. The leading arenas are described by William Hone in 'The Table Book', 1827, as two circular buildings, humble imitations of ancient Roman amphitheatres. One bore the inscription 'Bowll Baytyng', the other 'Beare Baytyng'. They stood in adjoining fields and appeared well-appointed for the reasonable off-duty comfort of the contestants.

Bear-baiting, like baiting the bull were sports under Royal patronage. When Queen Mary I visited Princess Elizabeth at Hatfield, it is said 'their Highnesses were right well content' with the great exhibition of bear-baiting provided for them, and when Queen Elizabeth entertained the French ambassadors on the 25th May, 1559, and the Danish

Bear-baiting at Charley's Theatre at Westminster in 1820, from Egan's *Real Life in London* (1821).

ambassador at Greenwich in 1586, they were amused by a display of bull- and bear-baiting arranged for their benefit. When James I became king, the Bear Garden came under Royal protection, the 'Master of the Bears and Dogs' appointment being given to Edward Alleyn, who succeeded Sir John Darrington in 1600. This position brought the holder as much as £500 per annum, although *officially* the actual fee attached to the office was no more than a farthing a day. Alleyn was succeeded by Sir William Steward on the accession of Charles, and the latest patent granted was to Sir Sanders Duncombe in 1639, who received the sole right of fighting and combating animals in England for fourteen years. The office was absolished in 1642. After the Restoration, bear-baiting came again into vogue, the pastime continuing on until the reign of Queen Anne.

With the decline of the sport following Queen Anne's reign, both bear- and bull-baiting had almost disappeared as a part of English life by 1750. However, some revival of the game was noted by William Hone in his *The Table Book*, 1827, in Duck Lane, Westminster, indicating that it was not wholly suppressed even in that year.

Badger-baiting

This pastime is perhaps more popularly known as badger-drawing, for the task of the dog was to 'draw' the badger from its box or hole which had been dug for it by its captor. Today the badger is fast disappearing from our countryside due to the encroachment of urban development on his natural territory. However, Hackwood tells us that at one time, the large numbers of badgers required for baitings in Birmingham were easily supplied from nearby Sutton Woods up to 1830.

It was usual to keep the badger captive in a box which was stored in a loft or cellar. The box would be about 60cm (24in) square, covered at the top with wire netting. Attached to the side of the box would be a tunnel about 3m (10ft) long. A light would be suspended over the top of the box so that both combatants could see each other while engaged in the skirmish, as could the wagering sportsmen present. As soon as the dog was brought on to the scene he would make straight for the open end of the tunnel, enter it and rush through to where the badger lay in wait. He would attempt to grab the badger and desperate struggle would ensue with the dog trying to draw his adversary through the tunnel into the open room. Perhaps the dog would get the badger halfway along the tunnel, only to be forced to retract to the box due to the badger's punishing bite. It is purported to bite at least as hard as a Staffordshire Bull Terrier and is certainly faster. Once taken hold he would tear back and many a good dog lost his nose and part of his muzzle in such a fight. One hears of Staffordshire Bull Terriers who could overcome

'Badger-baiting', as
published in Ackerman's
New Sporting Magazine
(1 February 1844) by W. B.
Scott after H. Alken.

badgers easily, but such dogs were few, I believe. A tough dog might well have achieved this with a badger which was physically sick or mentally dispirited by captivity, or more likely at a point of utter exhaustion due to continual rough handling by dogs which had been put at him earlier. However, point for point between two combatants, a 12kg (26lb) badger could usually put paid to, or at least deter, a much heavier Staffordshire Bull Terrier.

As is usual in these unpleasant sports, atrocities were common. Some unfortunate badgers would have the lower portion of their jaws cut away so as to render them unable to damage some cherished dog which might be used to draw them. Occasionally, badger-drawing was conducted in the open. The badger would be dug from his natural sett and another hole dug some four feet deep into the side of the bank of earth. At the far end a stake would be securely placed, then the badger's tail would be split, a chain passed through it and fastened to the stake. The dogs would then be brought in and set upon the badger one by one, who would then probably kill a few of them before he himself was mercifully despatched. In Scotland, badgers were frequently kept in the cellars of public houses for baiting, one of the popular rendezvous in Edinburgh being the 'Royal Mile' between Edinburgh Castle and Holyrood Palace. It is said that some badgers became so shrewd that, rather than suffer punishment, they met the dog halfway down the tunnel and allowed it to drag them quietly from the box without resistance!

Lion-baiting

It would appear that most of the incidents which involved the baiting of lions proved failures, but they were successful as crowd drawers. The first lion-bait was arranged by James I in the seventeenth century, the second by a menagerie proprietor named Wombwell in the nineteenth century. The 'Royal' promotions were arranged at the Tower of London on the 23rd June, 1609, and again in 1610, but in both cases the lions involved refused to show any active interest in the proceedings.

The Wombwell lion-baitings took place in 1825, the first on the 26th July, the second later in the same year. Much publicity was given to these events which were held in Warwick and large posters were exhibited in Birmingham, Coventry and Manchester, as well as all nearby towns. The lion involved, one 'Nero', tame and owner-bred in Edinburgh, was quite docile and apart from doing his best to defend himself from the three dogs, 'Captain', 'Tiger' and 'Turk' set against him, put up what appeared to onlookers only a playful attack. The lion certainly did not bite any of the dogs, but the damage done by his claws fending off the dogs maimed 'Captain' and 'Tiger' who crawled from the cage. 'Turk', the lightest of the three continued the attack, but was seized and laid upon by the lion, twenty times his weight. He was removed from the battle at last in very poor shape, but proved a game dog, as far as the onlookers were concerned.

The newspapers of the day expressed public indignation against Wombwell for his exhibition, but notwithstanding this the showman staged another bout, this time with 'Wallace', another Scottish-bred lion and of a temper very different to that of the gentle 'Nero'. Six dogs, 'Tinker', 'Ball', 'Billy' and 'Sweep', 'Turpin' and 'Tiger' were to be set against him. When the attack commenced 'Wallace' was ready for them. With one paw clapped hard on 'Ball' he took 'Tinker' in his teeth. 'Turpin' a London dog and 'Sweep' from Liverpool were thereupon released allowing the former two to crawl from the cage. Both dogs were beaten within one minute by the irritated lion. Then 'Bill' and 'Tiger' were let in, but the latter refused to 'scratch' and 'Billy' just escaped with his life by being dragged to safety through the bars of the cage by his owner. This appears to have been the last lion-bait in England. These baitings were regarded by the public as examples of unwarrantable cruelty, probably due to the fact that the spectators had the impression that the lions were too gentle, too kindly to be put to a baiting test.

At various times, the baiting of other animals such as the horse, an ape, an ape tied to the back of the horse, a polar bear, a she-wolf with cubs, a wild ass and a hyena, were conducted. None proved sufficiently interesting or attractive to the public and were never repeated.

Rat-killing

This was a popular sport in Victorian London. From the contemporary novel Augustus Mayhew's *Paved with Gold*, 1858, we learn much of the atmosphere, especially that in a pub called 'The Jolly Trainer' in a humble street off Haymarket. Here the landlord was one called Alf Cox, a retired light-weight champion pugilist and an inveterate dog man, accredited with the founding of the 'West End Spaniel, Terrier, small Bulldog, Bull Terrier and Toy Dog Club'. Although Alf was well known for his dogs he was also renowned for his weekly ratting contests held in the hostelry every Tuesday night. Silver snuff boxes and silver collars were put up to be 'killed for' by little brown English Terriers, Bulldogs and Bull Terriers, with an occasional Skye Terrier. Cox himself owned a good one in 'Tiny', whose performance of killing two hundred rats at a sitting was considered unequalled in the annals of ratting.

Betting, of course, was commonplace at these functions and the tavern was much patronised by young bloods of the gentry. The 'Great 100 Rat Match' was a highlight in Cox's ratting activities and it was well advertised by handbills and word of mouth. Mayhew describes the rat-pit as a small circus, some 2m (6ft) in diameter, about as large as a centre flower bed, with strong wooden sides, reaching to elbow height. Over it the branches of a gas-lamp were arranged, which lit up the white painted floor.

When one hundred rats had been flung into the pit, they gathered themselves into a mound, which reached one-third up the sides. These were all sewer and water-ditch rats, and the smell that arose from them resembled that from a hot drain! When all arrangements had been made, the second and the dog jumped into the ring or pit, and the former after allowing the Bull Terrier 'to see 'em a bit', let him loose. The moment he was free he became quiet, and in a most business-like manner rushed at the rats, burying his nose in the mound of fur, snapping and snuzzling until he brought out one in his mouth. In a short time a dozen rats with their neck wetted by the dog's mouth, were lying bleeding on the floor and the white paint of the pit became ingrained with blood. The dog was not completely unscathed either. In this particular match when four of the eight minutes allowed for the match had gone by, 'Time!' was called out, and the dog was seized by the backer, and forced to repose itself.

'BILLY'

Probably most famous in the annals of ratting is the celebrated rat-killing dog 'Billy'. He lived in the early 1820s and achieved fame by his remarkable exploit of killing one hundred rats in five and a half minutes, on the 22nd April 1823, this being his ninth match at rats. He was stated to have won with ease ten matches held between 1820 and 1823, six against time and four against other dogs.

He was got by Mr Pople's 'Billy', son of his 'Old Billy', bred by John Tattersal, Esq., of Wootten-under-Edge, Gloucestershire, from the best strain of Bulldogs in England. On the bitch's side 'Billy' was bred from Yardington's 'Sall', an extraordinarily good half-bred bitch from the 'Curley' strain and well-known to the fancy, and from 'Turpin', a Bulldog bred by J. Barclay, Esq., of Jacklin's strain, the greatest Bulldog fancier known in the world, and from 'Blind Turk', another famous Bulldog. These dogs have been traced back from the period for at least forty years by the oldest judges. 'Billy' killed many rats before he became known to the sporting world.

The Bulldog 'Billy' killing a hundred rats in five and a half minutes (1823).

'Billy' is shown in an engraving which was done to celebrate his exploit. This was published in London on the 23rd September, 1823, by S. Knight of 3 Sweetings Alley, Cornhill, London. He appears to be a white dog with tan ears and skull, busy at his task in the middle of the pit. With him is his owner, probably Mr Dew.

Although 'Billy' is referred to through his breeding as a Bulldog, it must be remembered that in this period, the term 'Bull Terrier' was new and only rarely used in the fancy. Most fighting dogs, whether rat-killers, dog-fighters or those used for the baiting sports, were known as 'Bulldogs' and even dogs weighing as little as 7kg (15lb) often fell into this category.

Dog-fighting

Dog-fighting was always a popular 'sport' but it came into its own as a more regular pastime about 1835 when the baiting of large animals such as the bull and the bear was forbidden in law. Pits abounded in the mining districts of South Staffordshire, Lancashire, Durham, South Wales, Scotland together with the London district and Ireland finding it very popular. The fights were staged in a regulation pit, across the centre of which was drawn a white chalk line. This was called the 'scratch' (the old bare-knuckle fighters had it too) and each contestant had to pass across it to attack his opponent in the opposite corner. A dog which would not do this was a dog which would not 'come up to scratch', thus losing the match either by his physical inability or cowardice, and sacrificing his owner's stake money at the same time. An owner seeing that his dog was losing the match could 'throw in the towel' as an alternative to allowing the dog to continue until he was so exhausted as to be incapable of winning, or to be killed. (It is interesting from an etymological viewpoint to consider the effect on our present-day English language of such phrases as 'top dog' and 'underdog'. They were once used to refer to the dogs' positions on the mat. And the term 'come up to scratch', which we use when we wish to indicate that a person has come forward to meet his obligations with courage, was used to describe a dog coming forward to fight. It is a sign when we note these terms, so popular in everyday use, that dog-fighting must have had widespread national appeal in those early days.)

Dog-fighting was an honourable pastime, at least so far as rules and regulations were concerned. The rules of dog-fighting remained un-changed for well over one hundred years. They comprised Articles of Agreement which had to be drawn up between the owners of both dogs, and duly witnessed by two or more people. It was usual however, that among men who knew each other well and respected each other's integrity that signatures were not demanded – their word was their bond. The following is the form of agreement used in the days of dog-fighting.

ARTICLES OF AGREEMENT

ARTICLES OF AGREEMENT made on the . . . . . day of . . . . .
18 . . . . .

. . . . . agrees to fight his . . . . .dog . . . . . pounds weight against
. . . . . dog . . . . . pounds weight, for £. . . . . a side at . . . . . on the
. . . . . day of . . . . . 18. . . . .

The dogs to be weighed at . . . . . o'clock in the . . . . . and fight
between . . . . . o'clock in the . . . . .

The deposits to be made as in hereafter mentioned; to be delivered to
. . . . . (who is to be the final Stakeholder); namely, the first deposit of
£. . . . . a side at the making of the match; the second deposit of £. . . . .
a side, on the . . . . . of . . . . . at the house of . . . . .; third deposit of
£. . . . . on the . . . . . of . . . . . at the house of . . . . .; fourth deposit
of £. . . . . on the . . . . . of . . . . . at the house of . . . . .; fifth deposit
of £. . . . . on the . . . . . of . . . . . at the house of . . . . .; which is the
last.

RULES

1st. To be a fair fight . . . . . yards from scratch.

2nd. Both dogs to be tasted before and after fighting if required.

3rd. Both dogs to be shewn fair to the scratch, and washed at their own corners.

4th. Both seconds to deliver the dogs fair from the corner, and not leave until the dogs commence fighting.

5th. A Referee to be chosen in the pit; one minute time to be allowed between every fair go away; fifty seconds allowed for sponging; and at the expiration of that time the timekeeper shall call 'Make Ready', and as soon as the minute is expired the dogs to be delivered, and the dog refusing or stopping on the way to be the loser.

6th. Should either second pick up his dog in a mistake, he shall put it down immediately, by order of the Referee, or the money to be forfeited.

7th. Should anything pernicious be found on either dog, before or after fighting in the pit, the backers of the dog so found to forfeit, and the person holding the battle money, to give it up immediately when called upon to do so.

8th. Referee to be chosen in the pit before fighting, whose decision in all cases to be final.

9th. Either dog exceeding the stipulated weight on the day of the weighing, to forfeit money deposited.

10th. In any case of a dog being declared dead by the Referee, the living dog shall remain at him for ten minutes when he shall be taken to his corner if it be his turn to scratch, or if it be the dead dog's turn the fight shall be at end by order of the Referee.

11th.   In any case of Police interference the Referee to name the next place and time of fighting, on the same day if possible, and day by day until it be decided; but if no Referee be chosen, the Stakeholder to name the next place and time; but if a Referee has been chosen and then refuses to name the next place and time of fighting, or goes away after being disturbed, then the power of choosing the next time and place be left with the Stakeholder and a fresh Referee to be chosen in the pit, and the power of the former one be entirely gone.

12th.   In the case of Police interference and the dogs have commenced fighting they will not be required to weigh any more; but if they have not commenced fighting they will have to weigh day by day at . . . . .lb until decided at the time and place named by the Referee, or if he refuses and goes away, then the Stakeholder names the time and place.

13th.   The seconder of either dog is upon no consideration to call his adversary's dog by name while in the pit, nor to use anything whatever in his hands with which to call off his dog.

14th.   To toss up the night before fighting for the place of fighting between the hours of . . . . . and . . . . . o'clock at the house where the last deposit is made.

15th.   The above stakes are not to be given up until fairly won or lost by a fight, unless either party break the above agreement.

16th.   All deposits to be made between the hours of . . . . . and . . . . . o'clock at night.

17th.   Either party not following up or breaking the above agreements, to forfeit the money down.

....

....

....

WITNESSES................................ SIGNED ....

....

The above rules, although somewhat primitive in their form and compilation, served well what many fanciers today view as a sport barbarous in the extreme. Nevertheless, like many things which go on and are disapproved by some it was a way of life in many parts of Britain. Even today, dog-fighting is said to be conducted in hole-and-corner places throughout the land. It is not unusual abroad and this writer believes that substantial sums are won and lost in its practice.

Some of the terms used in the rules will need to be clarified. To *taste* a dog is to examine him for any dressing applied to his coat. It was not unusual for unscrupulous owners to attempt 'nobbling' an adversary by rubbing in some obnoxious substance into a favoured dog's coat. An application of vinegar or a mustard and water mixture were popular. The adversary would be nauseated by the stuff once he had taken hold of his rival and put at once to a disadvantage. In the very early days of dog-fighting a 'taster' could be a man, who for the fee of possibly a shilling would lick over the dog's entire body to determine whether it had been dosed with anything! In later days, tasters would take two bottles of milk and a towel. One representative on each side would witness the purchase of the milk and examine the towel, for there were many tricks. The milk was used as a wash, then wiped over and cleaned off, so that nothing pernicious remained.

A *'fair go away'* is a term which indicates that both fighters' heads and forelegs are in opposite directions. The two dogs can then be picked up, thus ending the round. In such an instance, the dog which 'goes away' first, is the one which is expected to be the first to come to scratch in the following round, providing that it is a fair pick-up by the seconds. Should it not be a fair pick-up then each dog alternately comes up – no matter which dog makes the go-away. If, at the pick-up, one dog should catch hold of the other, both are again put down and the handlers (or seconds) wait for a fair go-away, as before.

Also in the 5th rule it was seen that with the call 'Make Ready' any dog which does not come up to scratch on the following cry 'Let go' or which stops on the way to the scratch line (say to raise his leg) loses the fight. Such hesitation was criminal to the dog-fighting fraternity.

Many a dog, reluctant to continue a fight so shamed his owner that he found himself sacked and thrown 'i'cut' (into the canal) on the way home. Many such dastardly acts have been perpetrated with dogs in the past. The worst thing was the ignorance which existed with many owners in those days. Scores of great-hearted, courageous and loyal dogs lost their lives because sadistic, greedy and drunken owners misused them, set them against impossible odds, fought them when they were ill, perhaps, or before they had recovered from an earlier battle or battles. Some of these men set their dogs to do what they would have been too cowardly to do themselves.

The true-blooded Staffordshire Bull Terrier fought because he wanted to. A dog cannot be coerced into a fight, especially if he lacks courage but then he cannot be termed true-blooded and a real Stafford. A dog fight did not carry quite the same degree of cruelty as a bear-, bull- or badger-bait. In such pastimes the baited creature did not have much option but to defend himself. A dog-fight in which the two contestants were evenly matched in body-weight and courage at least allowed for either one to give way if he so desired. In effect, one with such a mind would refuse to come up to scratch, thereby losing the fight and being withdrawn from combat.

The Staffordshire Bull Terrier or Pit Bull Terrier had his own fighting method. Some Staffords instinctively knew the tricks of their trade and could put themselves exactly at the centre of gravity of their opponent and throw him as quick as lightning. Some dogs were face-fighters, others fought for the legs – the forelegs generally. Some went for the ears, the sides of the face and the shoulder, but none was more dangerous than he who went first for his adversary's stifle. A stifle which has been crunched makes a crippled foe, one who cannot push in to attack and can scratch no longer – therefore a beaten dog.

Some dogs took a throat hold and this could be dangerous too, many lesser combatants giving up the ghost when they have been choked there too long. Some people think that a fighting dog, when he has taken hold will never let go. This is a fallacy. A proper fighting Stafford would seek for a better hold than the one he had, and hold only until he could find a better one – usually at the throat, which will often finish the fight. A fighting dog would fight a bitch. There are reports of matches in which a son fought his dam and she beat him! The *real* fighting dog is clearly undecided between love and war with a decided leaning towards war, so breeding of dogs possessing warlike strains needs careful attention – even youngsters of around four months can kill each other if left alone.

It was not unknown for a dead dog to win a fight! This might appear incomprehensible, but it sometimes happened. A dog, so ferocious and worked-up in battle may worry a dog which had already killed for ten minutes (see Rule 10). On breaking away, his second would pick him up and return to their corner. Then it would be his turn to scratch. Maybe because the living dog had reached his point of maximum effort, he had neither further heart nor physical impetus to move forward, unable to scratch. This would mean the dead dog had won!

Dogs were fought at varying sizes in the old days. Staffords used to range in weight from around 5.5kg (12lb) to beyond 27kg (60lb) in comparison with the present-day Stafford which mainly falls into a standard pattern of weight between 13.5kg (30lb) and 18kg (40lb). However, the breed has developed from an extremely wide concourse of combatant dogs, some small and usually employed in the rat pits, others of power and substance whose main function was against the bear and bull. Looks were of little importance – it was character that mattered. From such a stew-pot the varying weights arose. It was usual to match dogs in the pit according to their weights. Weight is of paramount importance in a fight which might continue for half-an-hour or more. Some fights went on for two hours – one in America extended to six hours, but this was unique, no doubt. Dogs were usually equally matched in weight, *slight* variance being acceptable. No one in their right minds matched dogs showing five or six pounds difference. Dogs would be matched at *fighting weight* and this meant they had to be in iron hard condition, no fat and their ribs visible. Owners used to go to extremes in their efforts to get their dogs down to a fighting weight – long walking on the lead up and down hills, vigorous jumping and leaping exercises, raw beef and oatmeal feeding and so on.

'Jem Crow' and 'Cartache' from an engraving by W. R. Smith after Cole.

London dog-pits

London abounded with dog-pits, most of them unsavoury. Some were constructed in the cellars of public houses; others were 'dives' where proceedings were conducted behind locked doors. The events were frequented by the 'swells' of Corinthian days in the middle eighteenth century and later. A notorious rendezvous was the Cock Pit, Duck Lane, Westminster. Other pits were managed at West Smithfield (the Gentleman's Subscription Pit), Windmill Street, Haymarket (Queen's Head Tavern), Peter Street, Westminster (the Elephant and Castle), Denmark Street, Soho (the Eight Bells) and the old Tottenham Court Road Pit. Noted sportsmen of their day such as Tom Crib and Jack Brown used to hold such meets at their respective pubs where not only dog-fights, but ratting, badger-baiting and cock-fighting were carried on. In these places gentry of both high and low denominations would cram behind the well-guarded doors and wager the outcome of the bouts. The 'swell' or 'spiv' of the day was invariably dressed immaculately. He is described in Pierce Egan's *Life in London*, 1821, also *Sporting Anecdotes*, 1820, and *Pierce Egan's Anecdotes*, 1827. Herewith an excerpt from *Annals of Sporting*, Vol.I, 1822 in which the writer speaks of the new breed of Bull Terrier, referred to by this name for the first time. He says:

> The new breed . . . as become so truly the go, that no rum or queer kiddy, or man of cash, from Tothill Street in the West to North-Eastern Holloway, far less any swell rising sixteen, with a black, purple or green Indiaman round his squeeze, the corner of his variegated dab hanging from his pocket, and his pantaloons well creased and puckered, must have a tike of the new cut at the heels of himself or prad.
> (The 'tike of the new cut' being, of course, the dog of 'the new breed')

Gentleman versus Bulldog

Dog and man fights were not unusual in the eighteenth century, and one such sport involved a man fighting a Bulldog with his bare fists. Both contestants were attached by chains to their respective stakes, the chains being of sufficient length to allow them to meet in the centre of the arena, but also enabling them to retire beyond each other's reach. From reports it appears that the man would not come out to the full length of his chain, whereas the dog wore himself out by continually lunging at him. The dog was eventually battered senseless, the man not coming off all that lightly, his hands and arms being badly ripped and mangled. A surprising report was announced over morning television in 1983 that a bout of this nature had been held in some clandestine fashion in Yorkshire! In spite of enquiries the writer was unable to obtain information on this remarkable news, but would welcome some details nevertheless!

Today, we live in more enlightened times with animals. The fighting or baiting of any animals is illegal, and while blood sports still exist, mainly in the form of fox-hunting, even this sport has an uncertain future. The RSPCA is, of course, strongly opposed to any activity which involves cruelty to animals and uses its quite considerable powers to convict and penalise offenders.

3 The Breed Standard

The Standard of the Staffordshire Bull Terrier is indispensable. It gives a word-picture of what is required in the breed and is, in effect, a target at which breeders must aim to obtain perfection in their dogs. Of course, there is no such thing (as far as this writer is aware) as a perfect Staffordshire Bull Terrier. There are good, even superb specimens, but these fall a little short of perfect.

The Standard was drawn up by a panel of breed pioneers and experts in their time. All these men, most of whom hailed from the Black Country, home of the breed and scene of its development, took on and completed their task in the face of much argument and rancour from certain fanciers of the day. However, two good specimens were selected as examples from the dogs of the day. These were Harry Pegg's 'Joe' (to become 'Fearless Joe') and Mrs J. Shaw's 'Jim' (to become 'Jim the Dandy'), red-fawn and dark brindle respectively. The pair were examined and discussed at considerable length, many measurements being taken and compared with individual weights.

It will be appreciated that in these very early days there existed in the breed a wide diversity of types and sizes. Some were as light as 10kg (22lb) and of distinctly Terrier type – others topped as much as 27kg (60lb) and possessed strong Bulldog tendencies in their heads and bodies. Naturally, their owners contended that these were the 'right' Staffords; even today some owners are perhaps inclined to consider that their geese are swans and this point of view is not always an easy one to override. To dampen the opinions of these objectors was to lessen their enthusiasm and possibly to lose their support and membership of the club. In that day, with numbers few, this could not be allowed, so careful handling of the situation was the order of the day. Eventually, a Standard was formulated which was acceptable to the majority and this was passed to the Kennel Club for approval. It was approved by this body and although it has been changed a little and modified since 1935, the current rendering is reproduced herewith by kind permission of the Kennel Club. Official copies are obtainable at the Club's London address (see Appendix) on payment of a nominal fee.

The Standard

CHARACTERISTICS: From the past history of the Staffordshire Bull

Terrier, the modern dog draws his character of indomitable courage, high intelligence and tenacity. This, coupled with his affection for his friends, and children in particular, his off-duty quietness and trustworthy stability makes him the foremost all-purpose dog.

GENERAL APPEARANCE: The Staffordshire Bull Terrier is a smooth-coated dog. He should be of great strength for his size and, although muscular, should be active and agile.

HEAD and SKULL: Short, deep through, broad skull, very pronounced cheek muscles, distinct stop, short foreface and black nose.

EYES: Dark preferable, but may bear some relation to coat colour. Round, of medium size, and set to look straight ahead.

EARS: Rose or half-pricked and not large. Full drop or prick to be penalised.

MOUTH: The mouth should be level, i.e. the incisors of the bottom jaw should fit closely inside the incisors of the top jaw and the slips should be tight and clean. The badly undershot or overshot mouth to be heavily penalised.

NECK: Muscular, rather short, clean in outline and gradually widening towards the shoulders.

FOREQUARTERS: Legs straight and well-boned, set rather wide apart, without looseness at the shoulders, and showing no weakness at the pasterns, from which point the feet turn out a little.

BODY: The body should be close-coupled, with a level top-line, wide front, deep brisket, well-sprung ribs, and rather light in the loins.

HINDQUARTERS: The hindquarters should be well muscled, hocks let down with stifles well bent. Legs should be parallel when viewed from behind.

FEET: The feet should be well padded, strong and of medium size.

TAIL: The tail should be of medium length, low-set, tapering to a point and carried rather low. It should not curl much, and may be likened to an old-fashioned pump handle.

COAT: Smooth, short and close to the skin.

COLOUR: Red, fawn, white, black or blue, or any of these colours with white. Black-and-tan or liver colour not to be encouraged.

WEIGHT AND SIZE: Weight: Dogs, 13–17kg (28–38lb). Bitches, 11–15.5kg (24–34lb). Height (at shoulder): 35–40.5cm (14–16in), these heights being related to the weights.

FAULTS: To be penalised in accordance with the severity of the faults: light eyes or pink eye-rims; tail too long or badly curled; non-conformation to the limits of weight or height; full-drop and prick ears; undershot or overshot mouths. The following faults should debar a dog from winning any prize: pink (Dudley) nose; badly undershot or overshot mouth. (Badly undershot – where the lower jaw protrudes to such an extent that the incisors of the lower jaw do not touch those of the upper jaw; badly overshot – where the upper jaw protrudes to such an extent that the incisors of the upper jaw do not touch those of the lower jaw.)

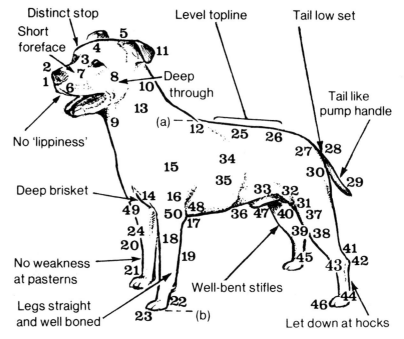

FIG. 1 The visual points of the Staffordshire Bull Terrier

1. Nostrils.
2. Nose, black.
3. Stop.
4. Skull.
5. Occiput – bone at the back of the skull, where the neck joins the skull.
6. Lips.
7. Face – muzzle.
8. Cheek.
9. Throat – showing no signs of looseness.
10. Neck.
11. Ears – 'rose' or half-prick preferred.
12. Withers. The height of the dog should be measured from withers (a) to ground (b).
13. Side of neck.
14. Brisket – part of the body between forelegs and immediately in front of chest.
15. Shoulder.
16. Arm.
17. Point of elbow.
18. Outer face of forearm.
19. Back of forearm.
20. Front of forearm.
21. Wrist joint.
22. Pasterns – point at which the feet of a Staffordshire Bull Terrier turn out a little.
23. Toes of forefeet.
24. Inner surface of the forearm.
25. Back.
26. Loins.
27. Croup.
28. Set-on of tail.
29. Tail – sometimes known as stern.
30. Buttock.
31. First thigh.
32. Flank.
33. Side of belly.
34. Ribs and chest wall.
35. Position of lung.
36. Floor of belly.
37. Stifle joint.
38. Second thigh.
39. Stifle.
40. Inner side of second thigh.
41. Achilles tendon.
42. Hock point or heel.
32. Front face of hock joint.
44. Metatarsus.
45. Inner side of metatarsus.
46. Toes of hind feet.
47. Sheath.
48. Sternum or breast bone.
49. Chest position.
50. Front or elbow joint.

It is from this written description of the desirable dog that Staffordshire Bull Terriers are judged in the show-ring today. Excellent though the Standard is in revealing how the Stafford should look, it can only at best provide the outward, visible features of the dog. In effect, it tells us very little about the anatomy of the dog. So to achieve success in breeding and in judging, it is necessary to know what lies beneath his skin, his skeleton, the mechanism which actuates him and how his muscles work. It is important then to study every section of the description and interpret the Standard in relation to the individual dog.

FIG. 2 Typical Staffordshire Bull Terrier dog and bitch.

Interpreting the Standard

One way to do this is to borrow the best specimen you know and read the Standard in relation to him. As you read it, savour the component parts of the dog with the relevant sections of the written description, thus:

GENERAL APPEARANCE: This is a batch of mixed virtues, all good Staffordshire Bull Terrier points put together make a pleasing picture. The dog should show a regal aspect, teem with breed type, which is essential to a pedigree animal if he is to represent an ideal example of his breed. His conformation should be correct and he should stand firm and give a balanced stance. To be balanced the co-ordination of his muscles renders him a good mover. In effect, the lateral dimensions of the dog should mould pleasingly with the vertical and horizontal measurements. Equally, the head and tail should conform and contribute to the balance of the dog's outline. The Staffordshire Bull Terrier, a dog built on rather chunky, if lithe lines, makes a well-balanced specimen when viewed in profile and can be fitted into an imaginary square.

HEAD AND SKULL: The breed Standard demands that the Staffordshire Bull Terrier's head should be short, deep through, broad in skull, very pronounced cheek muscles, distinct stop, short foreface, black nose. The 'stop' is the depression between and in front of the eyes, approximating to the bridge of the nose in humans. The head of the Stafford is virtually the hallmark of the breed and it is regarded by breed fanciers as of immense importance. It shows the dog's innate strength and rugged beauty. When one thinks of a good Stafford, the strong, broad, short muzzle and bumpy cheek muscles contribute to the visual and basic conception of the dog as a fighting machine. The original 'Scale of Points', not used these days, allocated thirty per cent of the total points to Head and Skull. This percentage, although later reduced by five per cent, indicates the importance attached to this end of the dog.

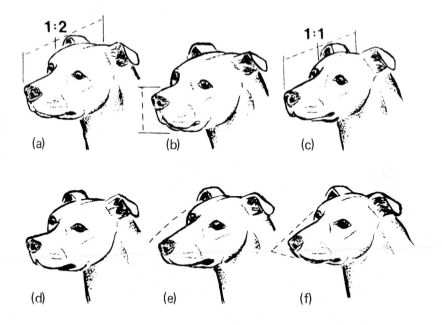

FIG. 3 Head types. (a) Typical. (b) Coarse head and muzzle with short foreface, lending itself to lippiness and underhung jaw. (c) Foreface and muzzle too long, lacking stop or indentation. (d) 'Dish-faced' – a concavity of the muzzle. (e) Down-faced – the muzzle taking a downward sloping course. (f) Snipy muzzle, i.e. a muzzle like the beak of a snipe – long, thin and pointed.

It has been stated by experts that an ideal proportion or balance of skull and muzzle is in the ratio of 2:1. It is necessary to have a solid, blocky, muscular head of great breadth and depth. The nostrils should be big (for sustained, deep breathing, essential in a dog bred to fight) and jet black (indicating good pigmentation). The occurrence of doggy heads on bitches and bitchy heads on males are both faults and should be penalised at least to some extent in adjudication, the latter fault being the lesser liked of the two. A good bitch with a doggy head would (or should) take second place in the show ring to a bitch with a head chiselled in feminine lines, other points being of equal merit. The Staffordshire's head should have considerable breadth across the top of the muzzle where it joins the skull. The distinct stop should be a major feature with

Dorelu Red Sam, owned by Mr and Mrs S. Lucy.

a head so made and the surface below the eyes should be well filled-in and the muzzle deep and strong. The shape of the muzzle and the development of the jaw muscles in a fighting dog are clearly of great importance. When viewing the muzzle in profile see that the repandus, which is the bent, upward part of the underjaw is plainly visible when viewed from the side, and not shallow or receding. There must be no tendency to snipiness with the muzzle; the top-line of which should be straight without evincing dish-face or down-face characteristics – all indications of weakness. A dish-face has a concavity in the top-line of the muzzle causing the nose of the dog to be tilted higher than the stop.

Dynamite Dempsey, owned by Mrs H. C. Hill.

Down-face is the opposite to dish-face (q.v.) when the nose tip is well below the level of the stop due to a downward inclination of the nose, this being a fault invariably accompanied by an overlong muzzle.

EYES: The Staffordshire Bull Terrier's eyes should be preferably dark, but may bear some relation to the dog's coat colour. Round and of medium size, they should be set to look straight ahead. The true Staffordshire Bull Terrier expression can be achieved only if the eyes are correct in colour, size and position. Each requirement plays its own part in contributing to this. The eyes of a Stafford tell the expert a lot about his character and his health, and so the eye should carry a glint and a distinct awareness. Although the Standard permits some relationship between coat colour and the eyes, there can be little argument against the superiority of a good *dark* brown eye, and this with any colour coat. This is a Terrier breed and as such should possess a dark eye indicating intelligence rather than shrewdness which is so often imparted by light-eyed Staffords. Bulbous or protruding eyes are unwanted in the breed; apart from their vapid untypical expression, I am not convinced they focus in the correct manner of this breed, also in a fighting dog a protuberant eye is soon damaged. Correct positioning of the eyes has its own importance when related to expression; eyes being too close together giving a mean look and those set too far apart an empty gaze, again both untypical features of the breed. A loose eyelid showing the haw is also objectionable and can prove a nuisance to the dog himself for it can collect dust, grit or pollen, causing irritation and often necessitating treatment.

One of the faults mentioned about eyes in the Standard is pink eye-rims and these should be penalised in accordance with the severity of the fault. Pink eye-rims on any coat colour other than white or piebald are certainly objectionable and should be dealt with by the efficient judge according to their extent. However, any dog so marked that white abounds over his eye region is liable to have some pink on his rims. Cases have been observed having rims mainly black, others mainly pink and it is suggested that the wise judge will use discretion on this point when judging dogs with coats of parti-colour.

In the Staffordshire Bull Terrier, eyes should never be over-moist. This feature often accompanies dogs who have prominent eyes and is due to the excess passage of tears from the corner of the eyes down the side of the muzzle or face due to obstruction of the normal passage of tears down the tear-ducts into the nose. The dog has two main eyelids, upper and lower, but a third lid known as *membrana nictitans* is situated between the main lids in the eyes' inner corners. It performs the function of protecting the outer surface of the eyeball when the cornea is affected by some foreign body or pressure. Behind the eyeball is a pad of soft fat which acts as a cushioning shield to the eye in the event of a knock or blow. If a dog becomes out of condition, this fat will disperse causing the eye to sink and give it a hollow deep-set look.

EARS: The Staffordshire Bull Terrier's ears sould be rose or half-pricked and not large. Full drop or prick ears are to be penalised. Ears play an important part in the general appearance of the dog. They should be carried in an alert manner for badly carried and big ears detract at once from the breed's beauty. The best form of ear is the rose ear, which is neat and rather small and when folded back exposes the inner burr. In a fight, the Stafford can lay these ears right back to hug the side of his skull, keeping them well out of the way from an adversary's bite. Half-pricked and prick ears (you seldom see the latter these days), although giving the dog a sharp outlook, need to be small and perkily placed and not much bigger than cropped ears to give them any value compared with the rose variety. Semi-erect ears if not too large often get by in the show-ring, much depending on their size and the way they are carried. The reason for ears which have an erectness about them is due to some

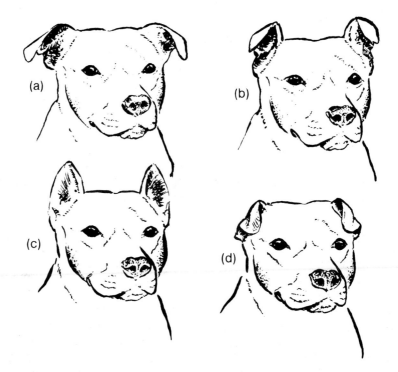

FIG. 4 Ear formations. (a) The typical 'rose' ear − preferred. (b) Semi-erect or half-prick ear − allowed and liked by some. (c) Erect, full-prick or 'bat' ear − unwanted. (d) Drop or button ear − bad type.

coarseness of the cartilage at the point where they join the skull. Drop ears are definitely out – they give the dog a hang-dog look and such ears are very vulnerable.

Ears should be fairly thin in texture, supple and of small to medium size. The important thing is that they should be tidy, for a dog can look good with ears a little larger than desired, providing those ears are well placed and nicely carried; they should also be well controlled.

The main purpose of cropping a dog's ears (now illegal in Britain since the Act in 1835, but never enforced until 1895) was to produce small, out-of-the-way ears which would not suffer in a fight. Many thought the cropped ears gave a dashing look to the dog and indeed this was true – some of the American Pit Bull Terriers one sees pictured certainly look smart. The business of cropping was a cruel one, no form of anaesthetic was used and more often than not the shears had to be used more than once to get the right shape and effect to the ears. The unpleasant practice persisted in Britain until 'Stonehenge' (the canine writer J. H. Walsh) protested about it in 1884. In 1889 the Kennel Club took up the question and before the end of 1895 an edict was passed that no cropped dog could be exhibited after the 31st March, 1895. This stopped cropping immediately. The rule was very unpopular with breeders of the white variety of Bull Terrier. The Bull Terrier Club of the day paid eight guineas for counsel and gave 'expert' defence at the hearing that a Bull Terrier could not live at all if it was uncropped! The Club lost the day and immediately did a round-about-face by petitioning the Kennel Club to prohibit the cropping of Bull Terriers and abolish the exhibition of cropped dogs!

There is no doubt that, if cropping was allowed in Britain, the Staffordshire Bull Terrier would be one of the first breeds to have its exponents of the 'art'. It is a pity however, that cropping is allowed anywhere in the world, for apart from the cruelty inflicted upon the poor dog, it is a sad comment on the breeders who cannot *breed* small, erect ears if they want such on their dogs. The old Bull Terrier breeders proved this. With the abolition of cropping, Bull Terrier breeders came to look at their dogs and found them with big, floppy ears. Within a decade or two they had started breeding out the big leathers and were producing small, neat and pointed ears. Today, it is to their credit that such ears are virtually fixed in their breed.

MOUTH: The Staffordshire Bull Terrier's mouth should be strong with teeth which are level and white. The bite should be of the scissor variety, i.e. with the top incisors resting over and upon the lower incisors with no space between. The lips should be tight and clean. In show judging the *badly* undershot and *badly* overshot mouths are severly penalised. Unfortunately, it has come about that some judges have inflicted heavy penalties on mouths which although undershot or overshot cannot be fairly termed bad examples of the faults. It is clear in the minds of most Staffordshire Bull Terrier breeders that a clean scissor-bite, level, Terrier mouth is the ideal. No one wants the typical Bulldog undershot jaw formation to be encouraged in spite of the fact that our Stafford's ancestors were clearly predisposed to such a mouth. However, it is necessary to appreciate, quite finely, in judging, the severity of the fault of the undershot mouth. A *badly* undershot or overshot mouth is one with a distinctly *visible* gap or channel between the upper and lower incisors or front teeth. This should be apparent when the dog's lips are lifted to examine his teeth, although in severe cases it will be suspected before this from the prominent or protuberant jaw formation when the mouth is closed – such a formation constitutes a critical fault and may be penalised at the judge's discretion. However, if the mouth is only slightly out of line then, although a fault, it would hardly justify the heavy penalty imposed upon it by some judges who seem only too ready to damn an otherwise excellent specimen on this fault alone. Slightly undershot mouths (you do not come across the truly overshot variety much these days) are faults comparable only with such as bad ear shape and carriage, gay tails and tight shoulders, or in fact, any fault, and should be penalised according to their severity – no more, no less.

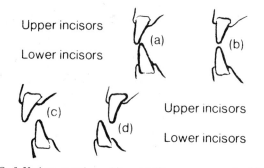

FIG. 5 Various mouths or bites. (a) The correct mouth. (b) The 'flush' mouth – not satisfactory. (c) The overshot mouth. (d) The undershot mouth.

It can be stated that the undershot mouth is a transmittable fault in pedigree breeding. This is true, but then so are almost all other physical faults and temperamental deficiencies. Too many judges see no further than the mouth of the dog. This does not mean that bad mouths are condoned, but a judge, if his opinion is to be worthwhile, must be able to assess the degree of misalignment in an exhibit's dentition and should be trained to give a fair balance of assessment. Clearly, in the show ring, a good dog with a level mouth must beat a good dog with an undershot mouth, all other points being meritoriously equal. It is obvious that every conscientious breeder should strive to disperse the bad mouth faults whenever they are seen and produce stock with the proper Terrier mouth. This type of mouth both cuts and holds well. The undershot mouth can hold well too, but it is not quite so foolproof in its mechanics for seizing and it is a bruising mouth of inferior worth. The 'flush' mouth, where both upper and lower incisors close tip-to-tip, and the 'wry' mouth, where the upper and lower incisors cross each other obliquely, are probably the two worst forms of mouth a Stafford can possess. These, by virtue of their formation, possess no cutting or scissor action whatsoever; further by virtue of the fact that top and bottom incisors rub and grind together, the dogs who have such mouths soon acquire eroded teeth.

Textrix King Oberon, owned by Jane Wheaver.

Dogs with missing teeth will lose points in a show. The odd one lost is of no great concern, unless it is a canine tooth which represents a useful dental armament in a Stafford. A judge needs to form his own conclusions regarding such matters which must be extremely variable. In domestic dogs, the number of teeth present is forty-two. Each tooth is made up of a crown seen above the gum and a root. The upper jaws contain six incisors, two canines, eight pre-molars and six molars. A puppy is born with permanent molars in the rear of the mouth. The pre-

Teutonic Warrior, owned
by Joyce Shorrock and
D. Rivenberg.

molars are changed during puppyhood over a six-month period and
replaced by permanent pre-molars. The largest cheek tooth in the upper
jaw is the fourth pre-molar (the carnassial tooth), which is changed later
for a permanent tooth. The corresponding tooth in the lower jaw is the
first large molar which remains throughout the dog's life. The canine
teeth are the largest, the part lying unseen within the jaw-bone being
nearly two and a half times as long as the visible portion. The incisors, or
front teeth, are placed closely together and increase in size from the
centre outwards in each half of the jaw-bone.

NECK: This is made up by the seven vertebrae of the spine running
from the head to the beginning of the backbone. The Staffordshire Bull
Terrier's neck should be rather short and strong with a distinct muscular
arch from occiput to point of entry at the shoulders, with appreciable
widening in this area. A good head should have a powerfully muscled
neck to support it, for however typical and beautifully conformed the
head may be, its effect is nullified if the neck is weak and unable to direct
its action. An overlong or 'ewe' neck lacks strength. One which is too
short lacks striking power and often carries loose skin and dewlap. Both
extremes militate against the balance of a show-dog specimen and the
physical prowess of a fighting dog.

FOREQUARTERS: The Staffordshire should have forelegs straight and well-boned, being set rather wide apart, but without any looseness at the shoulders or any weakness at the pasterns or wrists, where the feet should turn out a little. Fore-legs need to be wide apart to allow for wide and deep chest development, which should be muscular and fashioned to fit into the dog's picture of perfect balance from the front, this being just as important as balance assessed from the side. The legs need to be of correct length, not too long and not too short, for in a Stafford either extreme will affect adversely his agility and poise, points often overlooked by those who favour the ultra low-to-ground type of dog. There should be moderate shortness between the patella (knee-cap) and pastern (wrist), contributing thereby to good stance and movement.

The typical front is built on comparatively straight lines, broken at the pasterns and the chest, as seen in Fig. 6(a), is solid, fairly wide and muscular with evidence of great depth. A tight front, such as a typical Terrier (say a Fox Terrier) might have, is undesirable in a Stafford; this will be due to upright or 'proppy' shoulders and is often accompanied by a shallow or concave chest. Elbows which point out and away from the

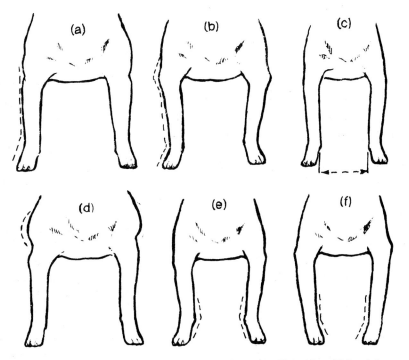

FIG. 6 Fronts (a) Typical front. (b) Out at the elbows. (c) Tight front. (d) Loaded or 'bossy' shoulders, i.e. shoulders with tight bunched muscle. (e) Chippendale front. (f) In-toes or pin-toes.

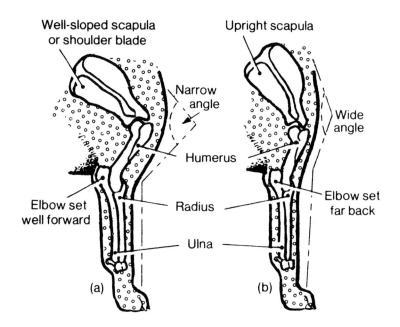

FIG. 7 (a) Well-sloped shoulders. (b) Upright shoulders.

chest wall are often accompanied by loose shoulders which protrude outwards, giving a false impression of extra width in front. Both these features are bad faults in the breed and militate against an individual's soundness. Sometimes a muscularly made dog is loaded with muscle at the shoulders which is not a particularly bad fault. Such shoulders are referred to as 'bossy' and often deceive an inexperienced judge who may think the specimen is powerful in shoulder. However, this is an inferior formation to long, well-toned muscles which possess more stamina and give a cleaner, visual front. The old-fashioned 'Chippendale' front is a weak front with the front limbs well bent in from the straight as in the furniture which bears that name. This is a bad fault. A weak foot formation which detracts considerably from a pleasing front is that which bears the name 'in-toes' or 'pin-toes' with the toes turned in to each other. This bad fault is usually accompanied by elbows which stand away from the chest wall.

BODY: The Stafford's body should be close-coupled, with a level top-line, wide front, deep brisket and well-sprung ribs being rather light in the loins. As in most Terrier breeds, the Staffordshire Bull Terrier requires a short back. However, one must understand the meaning and value of the short back. One which is too short tends to be rigid, therefore lacking suppleness, an important factor in an active breed. In all cases a back should be powerful and well reinforced with a muscular loin. The vertebral column of the dog needs to be very flexible to allow freedom of movement and for freedom in action. The breed Standard points to the desirability of a short back and, in fact, most fanciers consider the shorter the back, the stronger it is. However, there is no weakness in a longer lumbar formation providing the couplings are strong and ample muscle abounds the region. The *real* factor of worth in a short back is not its overall length, but the gap between the rear and hindmost rib and the pelvis, in other words, the loins. If this gap is too wide in relation to the size of the dog there exists and is a very marked impression of weakness. It is the closeness of this coupling which sets the seal of value on a short back and should it not be present the rear half of the dog appears divorced from the front region. Anatomical factors at either end of the specimen make their own contribution also. A well-joined neck to body, also a well set-on tail, will make a back *look* shorter and a dog formed with such attributes in moderation, providing he has adequate elasticity, will be found to have a natural, easy movement.

The top-line of a Staffordshire Bull Terrier's back should be level.

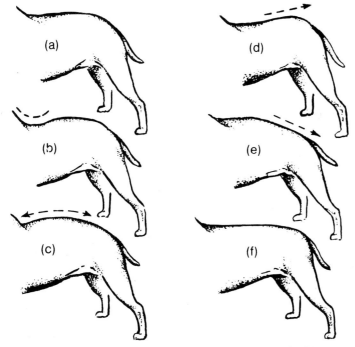

FIG. 8 Top-lines. (a) Conventional top-line, i.e. fairly level with some muscular undulations when viewed from side. (b) Sway back. (c) Roach back. (d) Stern high, caused by abnormal arching of the spine. (e) Sloping croup. (f) Long back − some allowances for long backs can be made in the case of bitches, but not dogs.

Keep an eye open for the unwanted 'sway-back', evidenced by a dip behind the shoulders, due to poor rib development or spinal defect. Another bad one is the 'roach-back', shown by a convex back-line, commencing with a line from a dip at the withers to another at the tail set-on. This abnormal arching of the spine is quite objectionable in the breed and is often accompanied by proppy shoulders. Lastly, there is the 'sloping croup'. This is usually seen in a dog whose tail is set-on too low. The croup is that part which covers the sacrum at the base of the tail and if the angulation of the sacrum and pelvis is in any case disharmonious, the dog under review will move badly and be at fault.

HINDQUARTERS: The Stafford's hindquarters should be well-muscled, the hocks let down nicely and the stifles well-bent. Legs should be parallel when viewed from behind. Powerful and well-angulated

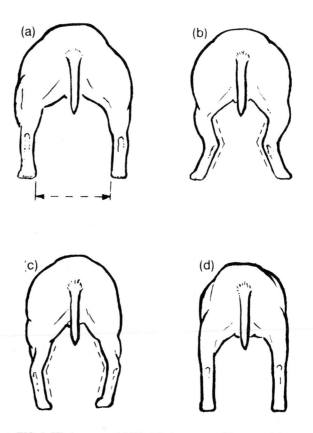

FIG. 9 Hindquarters. (a) Hind limbs set too wide apart giving an untypical gait. (b) Cow-hocks. (c) In-toed or pin-toed behind. (d) Average hind limb formation.

hindquarters are of vast importance to the breed. The old fighting-dog relied upon the strength of his hindparts to push in against his adversary. His opponent just as cannily sought to disable him there, and once this was effected, perhaps with one vast bite crushing the stifle, the battle was won for the biter. The dynamic thrust of a fighting dog lies in his hindquarters and every part of this propelling machinery needs to be well-oiled and moulded into the other. Well-bent stifles, adequately reinforced with muscular second thighs, operate the hind-limb quickly and effectively from a state of angulation to one of complete extension. Only by having elasticity in his movement, correctly fashioned bones of the right length and the muscles well-distributed and not bunchy, but rather long well-toned muscles, will the dog be able to maintain his staying power.

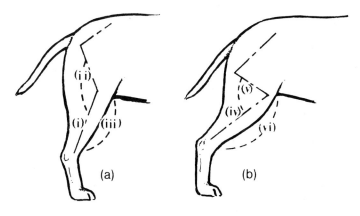

FIG. 10 Hind limb angulation. (a) Hind limb formation showing short tibia (i), and wide angle between tibia and femur (ii), and stifle (iii) being straight – limb lacks angulation. (b) Hind limb formation showing longer tibia (iv), and more acute angle between tibia and femur (v), the stifle (vi) being well-rounded or bent – limb is angulated (exaggerated for effect).

Other formations to look for include hind limbs which are set too far apart, giving an untypical gait. 'Cow-hocks' where the points of the hocks turn inwards, coming close together, causing the feet to turn outwards, which is an unsoundness and a bad fault. 'In-toed' or 'pin-toed' behind, this being the converse fault to cow-hocks; the points of hocks turn outwards, away from each other causing the feet to turn inwards when standing and moving.

The term 'angulation' used in relation to limbs is used to describe the relationship of bones to each other in forming joints and the angle so formed. When applied to the hind limb it refers to the correct angle formed by the true line of haunch bone, femur and tibia. In the forelegs, this would be the line of shoulder bone, radius bone and humerus. Lack of angulation suggests straightness in these joints. Quite apart from the Standard of the breed or breed points of the Staffordshire Bull Terrier, it is doubtful whether any specimen lacking even a slight degree of angulation could be considered truly sound. At one time, it was quite common to see dogs with their stifles straight. The stifle joint is the 'knee' joint on the hind leg and this is similar to the knee in the human. Straight in stifle is a term used to describe a hind limb in which the socket (into which the knuckle fits) is too shallow to hold the ball in place. This causes it to slip, with some pain to the dog and making lameness. The lameness is normally only of a temporary nature, but nevertheless, is capable of losing a good dog a prize award if it occurs while he is being exhibited.

The stifle is a complicated piece of anatomy – it includes a free-moving bone, the patella (knee-cap) which is quite small and is situated in its forepart, which normally glides between the two ridges and a central channel at the lower end of the femur. The inner ridge should be the slightly higher of the two and, with the bone formation being normal, this would be calculated to prevent the patella slipping. However, in

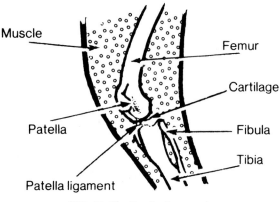

FIG. 11 The Patella (knee-cap).

certain selectively bred strains, there exists a tendency for both ridges to be equal in height and for the patella to slip, causing the dog to 'hop' with one or even both hind legs, sometimes in pain. This often occurs with dogs who are described as straight in stifle (see above). It is a frequent trouble with breeds which have been miniaturised and it occurs also with small Staffordshire Bull Terriers – dogs in the 13.5–15.5kg (30–34lb) range – this being at least one argument against the production of miniatures in our breed. In some strains the tendency towards a deformity of the stifle joint exists; this is known as formotibial articulation and is usually accompanied by dislocation of the patella. The trouble usually shows itself when the puppy is four or five months of age, varying considerably in degree. In Staffordshire Bull Terriers it is not uncommon, but not a serious menace and although some owners have ventured to surgical aid to put their dogs back on to sound footings, this is really not necessary in Staffords, for often enough the dogs, as they mature and make sound muscle find the fault subsides, often disappearing entirely by the time the animal reaches eighteen months of age. It is stated that patella luxation (patella slipping) is hereditary. Straight stifles are certainly transmittable faults and loose and slipping patellas often go with them. It is as well to avoid the use of a straight-stifled stud dog in the breeding programme, and with such care you are unlikely to produce stock afflicted with this disturbing unsoundness.

Hip Dysplasia: No section on hindquarters would be complete without some reference, at least, to the subject of Hip Dysplasia. This is a genetic problem involving degeneration of the *acetabulum* (socket) into which the femoral head (knuckle bone) should easily ride. The disease is as old as the hills, in humans at least, and may well have affected dogs for centuries too. Some experts disclaim it as a congenital disease as it does not appear to be present in the dog at birth, although there is little doubt about it being hereditary. However, what is not apparent at birth may well be extant and this feature of the condition has to be considered.

As stated, it is a ball-and-socket problem and there exists considerable friction and erosion in the joint as the animal grows into maturity. As these stresses continue, lameness gets progressively worse.

It cannot be diagnosed without the support of correct analytical scrutiny of an X-ray plate by a competent authority trained to acknowledged high standards. The BVA (British Veterinary Association) manages a joint scheme with the Kennel Club, known as the Joint BVA/KC Hip Dysplasia Scheme and this lays down certain rules for procedure by veterinary surgeons. Details are available from the Kennel Club and these come with an application card for submission of the dog's particulars with radiograph for scrutiny. The scrutineers have a panel which sits monthly and they either pass the dog as being free from HD when a certificate is issued, or the dog is failed, whereupon a letter is sent to this effect. For borderline cases, a 'breeder's letter' is sent to the veterinary surgeon to pass on to the owner.

Fortunately, HD affects Staffordshire Bull Terriers very little. The disease is commoner in the longer-boned breeds, but this does not mean that a vigilant watch should not be kept for signs of it in individual animals. It is not possible to state categorically that a dog has HD without the support of a correct analytical scrutiny. If a dog is being examined in the show-ring and he stumbles at the turn around or hops at every other step, swings his haunches unduly when going away or evinces odd characteristics in his gait, then HD might well be suspected, although patella luxation may be contributory to such peculiarities of gait. However, guesswork is not conclusive and the situation must be confirmed. It can even be possible that a dog moving well may be dysplasic, as instances have occurred that radiographic examination of the hips has revealed HD in a form which does not cause lameness! Even so, only an X-ray plate which has been scrutinised professionally will reveal the truth.

It must be remembered that HD is a complex hereditary condition which must never be ignored or allowed to penetrate our breed as it has done others. Breeders must ensure that they avoid at all cost any individuals who are its victims.

FEET: As has already been stated, feet should be well-padded, strong and of medium size. The Stafford has a strong, supple paw. This should

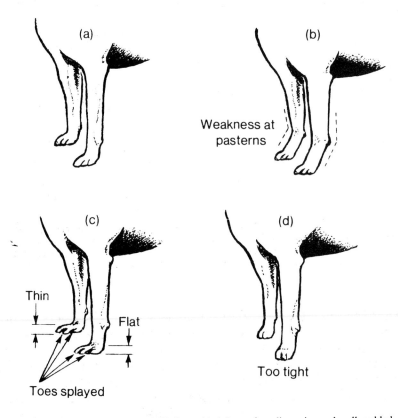

FIG. 12 Feet formations. (a) Well-moulded feet, of medium size and well-padded. (b) Down at pasterns. (c) Flat, thin feet. (d) Cat feet — close knit, tight-knuckled as required in the Bull Terrier, but not the Staffordshire Bull Terrier.

be well-knit, but not a high-knuckled tight foot like that of a cat. It should be sprung for instant and prolonged action. At the pasterns, the feet should turn out a little, and although this deviation away from the straight line of the forelegs is liable to offset a little the dog's forward movement visually; the feature is an important one to the fighting dog, for its typical, natural position allows for considerable freedom of action in all directions, pulling the body round to right, left and forward at will. Such a foot will also maintain for the dog good balance under stress and its formation can be likened to a half-hare and half-cat foot. The toes should be well split up with the knuckles quite prominent. Thin, flat feet and those with splayed and open digits represent a bad fault in a sporting breed of this kind. Remember too that a Stafford's pads should be deeply-cushioned, strong and resilient.

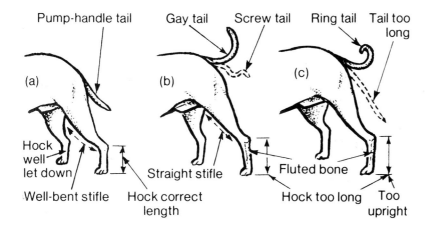

FIG. 13 Tails and Stifles. (a) Typical formation of stifle (well-bent and rounded) with pump-handle tail. (b) Straight stifle (lacking muscular development of second thigh) and so badly angulated. The gay tail and screw tail are both unsuitable. (c) Over-long hind limbs with fluted bone, indicating leginess. The ring tail and long tail are both undesirable.

TAIL: The tail should be of medium length, low-set, tapering to a point and carried rather low. It should not curl much and may be likened to an old-fashioned pump handle. The Stafford's tail is a distinctive one and contributes to his refined lines. In a scrap, a dog is inclined to slap his tail down on the ground and use its pump-handle end as a rudder to twist and swivel himself round to gain a better position to his advantage. A tail which is 'gay', i.e. which is high and up-in-the-air or curled above the level of the back, would not be much use for such a trick as this, quite apart from its lack of style and poor general appearance. A short,

Ch. Wardrum Dixie Queen, owned by Mr D. W. Smart.

cloddy tail detracts from a Stafford's balance, as does an over-long appendage. The correct length is usually indicated in a tail which measures barely to the point of hock. Tail carriage depends largely upon the angle or positioning of the sacrum in relation to the spine, the sacrum finishing where the root of the tail commences. The old sporting fraternity thought highly of correct tail, even to the point of believing that a tail which was too long pointed out its owner as a coward!

COAT: The Stafford's coat should be short, smooth and close to the skin. It is an individual coat as dog coats go, being one of the shortest kind in dogdom. Its texture is semi-harsh to the touch, being very pleasant to handle. The dog wears it very close-fitting to the muscles of the body and when he is engaged in combat or extreme exertion he will fill out his coat in a way which will make it grip him tighter and give his body an armour-like protection. This is why it is very difficult to grasp a fighting dog by the skin of his back or the scruff of his neck and indicates the need for a collar on your dog at all times. A dog's coat will give evidence of his condition. A smooth, flat-lying coat with natural lustre upon it will suggest a healthy animal. One with a staring coat along the spine is usually a dog which needs some attention. Long, coarse coats and those showing 'ruffs' are unwanted. Dogs which have been reared in very cold, Spartan conditions often develop long, untypical coats; those whose upbringing has been too warm and cosy, frequently grow coats which, although possibly short enough, lack the crisp feel which is so much admired.

COLOUR: The Staffordshire Bull Terrier's coat colour should be clear and definite. The approved coat colours are red and all shades down to fawn or fallow, white all over, white with black patches (piebald), white with brindle patches (skewbald), all the various shades of brindle or any of the reds, and brindles with white. Black-and-tan and liver colours are not to be encouraged.

Blue is an accepted colour, although it took some time (1950) before the breed recognised this coat. It is best likened to the blue of cobalt or to the greyish-blue colour of the pigeon. It comes in various depths of shade with occasional brindling and is singularly pleasing providing the pigmentation is intense and neither dilute nor fallowed. For best effect, it has to be accompanied by good dark hazel eyes and a black nose. Frequently, it turns up with blue noses, blue points (nails) and gooseberry-like eyes. When in these forms, it is not so attractive. The true blue is said to be the highest of its type in the evolutionary scale but it must not be confused with the weak and dilute coloured blue-fawn brindles which are sometimes seen. The gooseberry eyes referred to sometimes look like frogspawn or are periwinkle blue in colour; probably due to the breeding union of two diverse factors causing a partial or total reduction of the colour compound to its elements.

The Blue Paul: Possibly the source of the blue coat in the Stafford was the Blue Paul, a breed now extinct. It was used largely in the middle of the last century by the Scots for dog-fighting. Its colour is described as blue or blue-brindle – similar to that sometimes seen in Greyhounds. Legend has it that the breed was imported from abroad via Galloway, possibly by the pirate Paul Jones, which may account for the name. Some contend that the dogs were known as Blue Polls, because blue was the colour of their 'polls', i.e. heads. It is said that the breed was used by the Glasgow contingent and by gypsies in early dog fights and was bred solely for this purpose. Pedigrees (as with the early Staffordshire) were always verbal, never written, and little was cared about a dog's antecedents so long as he could win a match; winner being bred to winner. Various Scottish authors have described the Blue Paul and fight challenges may be seen advertised in early issues of *Bell's Life*. Many of these matches were held in the Burnside areas of Rutherglen and Baillieston up to the early 1890s. From the description of these dogs given by last-century historians it appears that the 'standard' of the Blue Paul was quite similar to our Staffordshire Bull Terrier apart from weight and size, the former variety being preferred at around 51cm (20in) at the shoulder and being fought usually around 27kg (60lb) in hard condition. The eyes are described as dark hazel, neither sunken nor prominent, no white or haw to be visible; expression rather comical, due

Belle of Burluraux, owned by Mrs M. Milner.

Cradbury Lady Flash, owned by Mr Fred Phillips.

to contraction of the eyebrows, evidenced when the dog's attention is rivetted. The description of around the eyes was supposedly peculiar to the Blue Paul, but some modern Staffords show similar optical characteristics. From an examination of this blue variety it is clear that it bore close resemblance to our modern breed and it may well have featured in the production of same. It is on record that the Blue Pauls produced occasionally some brindles and reds, the latter being known as Red Smuts in Scotland as they were not clear red in coat, but red-fawns with heavy spinal brindle tracings. Possibly the demise of the Blue Paul was hastened by the advent of the smaller fighting Staffordshire which fought in those days at 9–11kg (20–24lb) offering a sportsmen a faster, more varied and lively bout than did the much heavier sort.

All coats should be of good, intense pigmentation. Reds are particularly attractive with black facial masks, black eye-rims and black toe-nails, all these setting a good seal of proper colour in the dog. White dogs are quite acceptable in the breed: in fact, many really good ones have been so coated, both in the pit days and during the exhibition period of the last forty-odd years. White Staffords with patches were even more common then than they are today. Often enough, it is difficult to produce white dogs with black eye-rims, which are desirable, many good specimens having rather pale, pinkish rims. When judging some elasticity should be observed with this factor and, in the author's opinion, penalisation can reasonably be avoided unless in very tight competition.

It is generally believed that by breeding such as red to red, colour pigmentation will weaken. In fact, the issue from such matings, if repeated, may well acquire coats of light fawn or even fallow-yellow. To guard against colour deterioration, it is recommended that an occasional cross to distinct brindle is introduced to a breeding programme. Paling of coat colour can be caused by breeding red to red or fawn to fawn for more than a generation or two. It can also be caused by some modifying factor which is effective in diluting the visual colour. Certain red stud dogs possess the ability, by virtue of the fact that they are of genetic construction which is entirely free from this modifying factor, to produce stock which is of their own good red colour. They are thus able to maintain a consistency of good colour in their litters. To find such dogs it is necessary to examine their issue at every opportunity. It will be found that some maintain good red sons and daughters and these should be the ones in use in preference to those who get a good percentage of fallows and similar light coats such as biscuit and lemon, assuming that these lighter coats are not admired, or specifically required by the breeder. It should not be overlooked that even a brindle of intense colour himself may carry the diluting modifier as a recessive and, by using him, deepening of colour in the progeny may well not be achieved. Even the reds in the second generation following a cross to the brindle stud dog can prove lighter in colour than any of their red predecessors. The foregoing indicates the importance of studying the progeny of stud dogs before introducing their blood to any breeding scheme.

WEIGHT AND SIZE: The Staffordshire Bull Terrier should weigh, in the case of dogs: 13kg to 17kg (28lb to 38lb); bitches: 11kg to 15.5kg (24lb to 34lb). When measured at the shoulders, the height should be 35cm to 40.5cm (14in to 16in); the heights being related to the weights. Quite wide extremes in both weight and height are shown and to the casual reader this might raise an eyebrow. However, it should be remembered that the Staffordshire Bull Terrier's confirmed breed Standard, although formulated in 1935 was not finalised until considerably later – at least as far as this section is concerned. Further, it is still a comparatively young breed as far as standardisation of type etc. can be fixed. Although quite old in its history, the interest in its set formation represents not much more than thirty generations of dog breeding development. Bearing in mind the very wide divergence of Stafford types which existed prior to 1935, it is hardly surprising that breeders have a long way to go before they can even hope to standardise every litter. In the early days, a wide range of sizes were available to support the first Staffordshire Bull Terrier breed shows. Dogs of 13kg (28lb) and less were commonplace, as were specimens which exceeded 18kg (40lb). In fact, records show that Staffordshire Bull Terriers, or Bull Terriers as they would have been if we look at them prior to Kennel Club recognition, sometimes fought at 6.5kg (14lb). Such a weight was a popular one with many of the 'sportsmen' of even the early part of this century. Consequently, it is not surprising that considerable leeway was allowed in the matter of height and weight. Had the wording of the Standard in this section been too rigid, many potential exhibits would have been deemed ineligible and the early shows would not have got away to the flying start they achieved, because both these dogs and their owners would have lacked interest and stayed away.

Today, breeders try to produce a dog which stands about 40.5cm (16in) at the shoulder and weighs around 17kg (38lb), although frankly an acceptance of 18kg (40lb) might have been a better choice, for such a specimen having this relation between height and weight would be rather more nicely balanced. Admittedly, no scales are seen today at Staffordshire Bull Terrier dog shows, otherwise it is certain that many of the eye-pleasing winners would be found to exceed the permitted 17kg (38lb) when they were weighed. In the beginning at some of the shows and matches, spring-balances, tape measures and rulers were occasionally noted in sometimes vigorous hole-and-corner arguments between exhibitors! Fortunately, these days, experienced show-goers assess such weights and dimensions with their eyes rather than resort to such impedimentia. Providing the dog is well-balanced then some marginal deviation from the permitted maximum weight of the Standard can be allowed. Slavish insistence to any detailed measurements will cramp the style of a judge and restrict his commonsense approach and interpretation of the Standard.

Australian Ch. Lydes Jaguar
of Linksbury, owned by Dr
L. Davidson.

Remember that a show dog has to be *adequately* covered in flesh
(unlike a fighting dog). If your dog is a big-framed specimen, then that
frame must be covered suitably. It serves no useful purpose to work off
the extra 2.25kg (5lb) of flesh from a 19.5kg (43lb) dog to bring him to
the requirements of the Standard. Providing that the amount of flesh he
is wearing is correct for his size then all you will do by reducing it is to
make him look thin and probably interfere with his visual balance.
Again, recalling past dog shows, I have seen owners with their
overweight dogs outside the show venues jumping their dogs up-and-
down and applying all forms of exertive exercises to them in an effort to
throw off a few pounds before entering the show ring – even at that late
hour. They might have only shed a few ounces, never mind pounds, in
doing this and thereby achieved nothing apart from making the exhibits
excited, exhausted and quite unfit to show properly. From my own
observances, it does not do too much good to the owners either! The
same applies to a spare tight-coated dog of say 15kg (33lb), whose owner
tries to get a few pounds substance on him just before an important
show; suet pudding and other stuffings do nothing except bloat the dog
and again ruin his balance. If you insist on a 17kg (38lb) specimen then
you have either to breed or buy one. It is useless to fine down or fatten
up those which, while good specimens at their weight, fall on either side
of that desired.

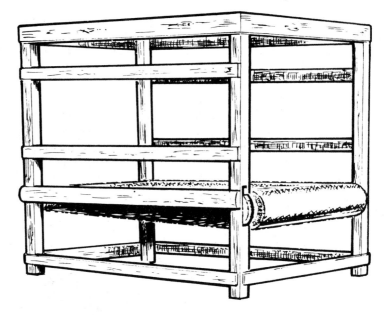

FIG. 14 A treadmill of the kind made by Colby of Newburyport, Mass., USA, for the last fifty years.

A useful contrivance for bringing a show dog into good hard condition, apart from walking him on the lead for considerable distances while on hard ground, is the treadmill (see Fig 14), which is used quite extensively in America. The idea is an excellent one once the dog gets used to the system. A frame or cagework is made of wood or steel; in the lower section of the cage is constructed an endless belt, rather like a conveyor belt, which, being ratcheted, will only move backwards. The belt itself is made of heavy-pile carpeting on close-knit wooden slats upon which the dog is placed, with his head held by the trainer or with his leash affixed securely to the top part of the cage. The dog is then encouraged to run forward, whereupon the belt begins to move and the dog gets his exercise without moving from the spot. John P. Colby, the well-known American dog man and brother of Joseph Colby, author of *The American Bull Terrier*, 1936, published in Sacramento, makes a very good noiseless model which allows the dog to make his own speed. Many of these treadmills have been sold to Pit Bull Terrier owners in the States over the last forty-five years and have proved successful in training a dog by exercise into hard condition. The sketch shows the form of this model which retails in the States today. Mr Colby's home is in Newburyport, Massachusetts.

FAULTS: Light eyes and pink eye-rims we have discussed already in the section on eyes; tails, over- and under-weights and size generally have been commented upon, as have mouths and ears. Left for us to consider as features which are taboo are the Dudley, or pink (flesh-coloured), nose and liver and black-and-tan coats. Liver coats are displeasing because the coat colour is usually associated with the undesired Dudley nose and pink-flesh eye-rims. Dogs of this colour are wont to produce litters which abound with such a colour and this is alien to the breed Standard. The black-and-tan coat is another variety coat colour which is not to be encouraged. The true black-and-tan markings are to be seen on the Manchester Terrier and its cousin the English Toy Terrier. These breeds have jet black glossy coats with rich mahogany tan on the muzzle to the nose, tan spots to the cheeks and above each eye. The underjaw and throat area are tanned with a 'V'-form and tanning is seen on the breeching and knees downward. In Staffordshire Bull Terriers the tan is seldom a rich-coloured marking, but more like a musty-fawn and the black far less dense than on the true black-and-tan. A judge should be sure of his ground in assessing whether the black-and-tan he is examining is in reality a marking to justify disqualification out of hand; or should it be categorised, perhaps unfavourably, with exhibits possessing conventional coat colours. To disqualify a dog in competition because it is black-and-tan, a dog should have the back, loins and parts of his head black or mainly so. His throat, cheeks, legs, breeching and under the tail should be tan or fawn. No one knows quite why this type of marking is taboo. It is known however, that black-and-tans and tricolours if bred, procreate the marking to excess and it maybe that the old-timers, seeing the danger involved with this, forbade black-and-tans in the Standard. The same hazard exists with liver coats and the erstwhile Dudley nose. Mahogany brindles are sometimes wrongly classed as livers, but any brindle dog with dark eyes, black nose and black points such as lips and eye-rims cannot be said to fall in that class.

Two factors of utmost importance which are not mentioned in the breed Standard are 'Type' and 'Soundness'. No Staffordshire Bull Terrier would be worth anything without both attributes.

TYPE: This is the quality which is essential to a Stafford if he is to represent or approximate up to the ideal model of his breed based upon the Standard drawn up by a body of recognised experts. A dog who 'has type' is therefore one who, although not necessarily perfect, embodies much of the ideal; conversely, a dog 'lacking type' is one who, though possibly in possession of several good points, is a long way from being the living model of his breed. Where exact breed type is established and this happy state is not yet the lot of our Staffordshire Bull Terrier, the fewer potent stud dogs the better in our breed. The sense of this is contained in the fact that it would make for a reduction in variation through an advance towards genetic purity and a wider distribution of

Ch. Cradbury Flash Danny Boy, owned by Mr Fred Phillips.

Ch. Benext Beau, owned by Mr and Mrs K. Bailey.

the dominant factors desired. Utopian results can be achieved only if all the faulty specimens which appear are *entirely* rejected for breeding. It is because genetic purification, or up-grading, follows the use of a few first-class stud dogs that type is often higher and more uniform in the numerically smaller breeds than in the more popular ones.

SOUNDNESS: A dog may have excellent component parts, but without physical orientation to fuse these into a pleasing whole, he *must* be unsound. On the other hand, it is feasible that an unsound dog could teem with type, for soundness is unaffected by type and vice versa. Type as such is not detailed in the breed Standard, as we have said, nevertheless it is an essential feature of the Staffordshire Bull Terrier, but it must exist with soundness. Soundness can be inherited or acquired. A dog, following an accident may be unsound. As long as he limps because his damaged leg hurts, it can be assumed that he is unsound. His temporary unsoundness is not thrown off until the pain stops and he stops limping. This type of unsoundness concerns us little, for it will not be passed on to the animal's progeny, being non-genetic. Soundness like type must be understood when interpreting the Standard, in spite of the fact that neither are mentioned. Anatomical unsoundness includes structural faults such as upright shoulders, which in a Staffordshire Bull Terrier would produce stilted action and probably coarse formation of the neck and thorax. Cow-hocks, where the points of the hocks turn towards each other, are often caused by muscular weakness, the second thigh or hocks being too long or even a general structural weakness. An exceptionally narrow pelvis would cause the exhibit to move too closely together when moving away. A rear view so presented is one lacking muscular strength, the effect of angulation is absent and the fault is normally one of generic origin, and being so, its effect can be lessened only by careful breeding. Loose elbows (out at elbows) are another generic fault and one certain to damn the chances and career of any prospective show or stud dog. This fault can be induced or acquired – either by rickets in puppyhood, probably due to faulty feeding and rearing with environmental restrictions, or bad lead training. A number of other physical unsoundnesses can occur in dogs. The more obvious ones are easily recognised, but unfortunately, some of them, such as acquired deafness and acquired, as well as inherited, eyesight failings, impotency etc., are not. These faults are normally left to the honesty and integrity of the owner (or vendor) to admit them, and it speaks highly for them that when recessive conditions have appeared in Staffordshire Bull Terriers, they have not been slow in revealing the facts for the benefit of the breed.

In effect, anything which impairs the soundness of a Stafford, whether this is permanent or temporary in nature, is an unsoundness. It *can* apply to a Staffordshire who is below par in health and condition, working efficiency, action or character. Many things contribute to unsoundness – bad positioning while in foetal form in the dam, the effect of transient local pressure and obstructed circulation, even faulty pre-natal feeding of the dam. In puppyhood unsoundness can be caused by faulty upbringing, even too much or too little exercise or the aftermath of a contractable disease. Any breeder contemplating the use of an unsound dog should examine very closely its history of unsoundness as well as its nature. It may well be that a dog with *acquired* features of unsoundness could prove a useful parent, whereas one with a genetic anatomical fault is quite useless in the breeding field. Remember, too, that soundness includes temperament and a vicious, unreliable dog, or one whose character is alien to that which is sought in the breed, can be rightly classified as unsound. Whether a dog has acquired or inherited features of unsoundness on the day of the show he has to be penalised.

BALANCE: Another feature not mentioned specifically in the breed Standard, but which is essential to the Staffordshire Bull Terrier himself as well as to the eye of a judge. It is the co-ordination of muscles, giving graceful action coupled with the overall conformation of the dog. In effect, the lateral dimensions of the dog should mould pleasingly with the vertical and horizontal measurements. Equally, the head and tail should conform and contribute to the balance of the dog's outline. The Staffordshire Bull Terrier, a dog built on rather chunky, if lithe lines, makes a well-balanced specimen when viewed in profile when he can be fitted visually into an imaginary square. When seen from any angle, the various parts of his physical make-up should fit the Standard and fuse correctly one with the other. His action or movement is controlled by balance; action being the manner in which the limbs are employed to propel the dog in his particular gait. The Staffordshire Bull Terrier has an individual style of movement, treading the ground neither wide nor narrow with his front feet, the limbs of the hindquarters showing some degree of parallelism when going away and with ample spring, stride and rhythm. The action of all four limbs has to be positive, neither weaving, ambling, fleeting, 'paddling' or the high-stepping style of action perhaps desirable in some other breeds but not in the Stafford. In this breed, obliquely set shoulders and well-let-down hocks are standard requirements and any specimen which is loose in shoulders, out at elbows or with upright shoulders and high hocks cannot possibly move in a typical manner.

To produce correct movement in the breed it is necessary, therefore, to fix both the structural details and pre-disposing nervous qualities genetically when arranging a breeding programme or in the normal selection of mates. Further, even a dog approaching perfection in these departments requires correct training in ring deportment and presentation if he is to express truly the action typical of his breed. Likewise, even tail qualities, i.e. correct length and carriage, should fit into the desired picture; no dog with his tail too long or too short, carried other than in the virile 'pump-handle' form required by the Standard can be expected to express correct breed action. A dog's temperamental balance must also be considered in the assessment of his physical balance. Any dog apathetic with indifferent health or boredom, i.e. lacking mental well-being, is unlikely to display his virtues in a pleasing manner and would thereby lose points in competition with another dog of quality points in superb mental health and fitness.

4 Breeding

Every lover of the Staffordshire Bull Terrier should wish to contribute to the breed's continual improvement. Breeding dogs is a fascinating and consuming hobby – quite often it proves rewarding. The production of pure-bred dogs conforming as near as possible to the current Staffordshire Bull Terrier breed Standard should be the goal of every Stafford enthusiast.

Very few dog owners either understand or, indeed, care much for genetics and certainly not many people can claim a knowledge of the subject. Those who do, learn one thing quickly – that it is virtually impossible to deduce a Staffordshire Bull Terrier's breeding potential from his or her appearance alone. It is equally impossible to do any more than guess at potential from pedigree alone. On the other hand, it must be admitted that some dogs teem with type and give the *impression* of latent virility, verve and power. Such as these are very often good begetters in the stock-breeding field and deserve more than a casual glance when unions are contemplated between dog and bitch.

The breeder has, in fact, only two clear factors to work with – one is appearance, the other pedigree. These two specifics, carefully calculated and intelligently analysed, will prove invaluable in an effort to improve upon his stock. Firstly, he *must* know how to read a pedigree. Dogs have faults (as has been said, there is no perfect specimen in the Staffordshire Bull Terrier world); some of these being serious and transmittable, others of little consequence and easily enough bred out. However, the serious faults require a more concerted attack on them to prevent their appearance in the progeny and this is where knowledgeable pedigree reading plays its part. To know each and every individual on the two pedigrees of a pair to be mated is ideal. Unfortunately, it is not always possible to obtain such specialized knowledge of the ancestry shown in these documents, although often enough a good deal of worthwhile information can be gleaned from old-timers in the breed whose memories can be persuaded to go back reliably down the past show years. It is a wise breeder who prepares a sort of dossier on every dog and bitch, where not only their names, but their bad as well as their good points will be revealed, and this advice applies not only to a dog's physical points, but to its character and propensities. To the owner of the dog in a proposed mating pair it may become apparent at once from such data why his dog lacks good ear carriage, or to the bitch's owner why his female carries her stern a fraction lower than the Standard

Ch. Northwark the Pirate,
owned by Messrs Consadine
and Frazer.

Ch. Worden Queen, owned
by Mrs M. Gilfoyle.

edicts. He may observe faults in the pedigree which appear in duplicate,
even in triplicate. One hopes that if he observes faults in the male's
pedigree which reflect the faults in his bitch, he would at once dismiss
the idea of bringing them together. Should he not heed such a warning

then he would be adding multiples of such faults to the breeding of the progeny. Maybe the foregoing example is sketchy, but no doubt it will serve to show the principle involved by studying pedigrees and co-ordinating the findings to animals of good appearance when striving to produce good Staffordshire Bull Terriers.

It is most important when perfecting one's stock to observe keenly and practise carefully in breeding. When preparing a pedigree for study, one of at least five generations should be used. With the annotations you inscribe against each name on that pedigree you will transform the dossier into something vital and revealing as to the probable breeding value of the animal studied. In effect, by examining the living Stafford you will ascertain the *visual* defects he possesses; by the study of pedigree you will discover the *hidden* faults he carries. The inter-related discoveries made must guide you when planning your next breeding programme.

Care must be taken, particularly if your research into pedigree extends back into the thirties and even more recently in some cases. Written pedigrees were rare in those days. Most of the Pit Bull Terriers, later to be known as Staffordshire Bull Terriers, had one name and that would probably be an abbreviated forename like Bob, Ben, Bess, Jim, Rose or Tip. With such names and it is true there were not many more in use, separation of the individual would be virtually an impossible task for the student. A further frustration is that many of these dogs were of unknown parentage, a feature of the casual attitude to dog-breeding in those days. Where a pedigree was required it was, unfortunately in some instances, speedily manufactured – this was something the Kennel Club was quick to stamp out when Staffords were recognised in their registry. Thus, many early pedigrees were not worth the paper on which they were written. Nowadays with all this confusion many years back and well and truly blanketed with the passing of time, we are able to look at good dogs and bitches and know something about their ancestry over perhaps thirty years of clean, honest breeding. The trouble is, that you cannot always find a mating pair which produce what you are seeking. In times gone by, good heads seldom went with sound action and it was far from easy to get progeny which amalgamated the two desired features. Today, with so much useful data available to breeders, the problem of point-fixing has been minimised considerably and the Staffordshire greets the world a better made and 'typier' dog than he used to be. The standard of quality being better, the competition in the show ring is keener, but it all gets our breed nearer to perfection.

Methods of breeding

LINE-BREEDING
To line-breed, the breeder aims to obtain the desired blood and

characteristics directly or indirectly by mating with descendants of the dog whose points attract him. To achieve this successfully, he will need to select very carefully and mate dogs who have certain excellent points to related dogs who have similar good points, possibly in moderation. This would normally be expected to improve upon and fix such points. It is common to mate dogs with the same sire and different dams and vice versa to conform to line-breeding rules, examples being the matings of grandson to grandmother, grandfather to granddaughter, nephews to aunts, nieces to uncles and half-brothers to sisters. Nevertheless, no such unions should be contemplated unless the pair to be mated are good specimens in themselves, show a distinct likeness to each other and, needless to add, are sound and healthy examples of the breed.

With this system, which in its way, is not dissimilar to in-breeding, but is much safer, one ancestor would appear twice in the previous three generations but not within the last two. The term line-breeding is often extended to include pedigrees in which one ancestor appears twice within the last five generations. Considerable care needs to be employed when using the method so that undesirable traits (recessives) are prevented from rising to the surface and becoming fixed. These recessives will make their presence felt if given the chance and then you will get atavism or reversion to early type which is just what you have been striving against.

Once a pure strain has been established by this system, not a lot can be done to improve it while the breeder continues to use his own stock. At this stage it frequently becomes prudent to seek and introduce new blood. Herein lies some danger, the dog to be used needing to be thoroughly vetted as far as his effect in breeding is concerned. It is wiser to use a sire whose worth in the breeding field has been already clearly and irrefutably established than to employ a dog, perhaps better in breeding and as a specimen, merely because of these attributes and economy. An untried youngster of such calibre might well ruin in no time the efforts of a breeder's lifetime. There is no difficulty in ascertaining what a stud dog has got in his career; show results tell most of the story and the people 'in the know' in the Stafford world are often the most successful exhibitors who can recount almost any stud dog's position in breed society, which is based on the quality and success of his offspring.

No two dogs are identical, even though they are of similar gene construction. I have no intention of getting on to the science of genetics, for this is a specialized field which has its own books and experts. However, those who wish to read a good book on breeding are advised to take *All about Dog Breeding for Quality and Soundness* (Pelham, 1978) by Jean Gould. It is apparent that as breeders become more obsessed with their subject that genetics then becomes a science to study and, no doubt about it, good results come from a close study of this somewhat abstruse subject. When slight variations in pure lines are noted, it can sometimes be attributed to environment. Such variations are therefore acquired or non-inherited as opposed to genetic. To mention only a few such effects one can consider fluted bone, splayed feet, loose shoulders, cow-hocks, puny structure and similar weaknesses, all the results of poor environment and possibly ill-treatment. Such faults, as they are, are not necessarily prone to affect an animal's progeny, providing that they were acquired during that animal's development. The ordinary process of selection need not be affected by them. On the other hand, dogs who show the effects of undesirable mutations must be disposed of immediately for they can contribute only harm to the strain. Undesirable features of any sort must be eradicated as soon as they are noted. The only stock to keep is that which can maintain the good standard of the strain you have aimed at.

IN-BREEDING

This is strictly involved with the planned mating of related dogs in order to perpetuate certain characteristics which may be desirable, and which already exist to some extent. For examples of in-breeding, one would mate together father and daughter, mother and son, brother and sister. Such a method of breeding is only for knowledgeable and experienced breeders. It holds, as a practice, many dangers and pitfalls – for while it may well fix and cement good points, it is equally likely to do the same with bad points, some of which may well be latent (and probably unknown by the breeder) in the parents and their ancestors. Close breeding can prove responsible for infertility, cryptorchidism or monorchidism in future generations. It is useless to hope for anything but failure if in-breeding is practised with chance-bred or mediocre stock. The animals used *must* be of high general quality and free from defects in the widest sense. Unless such material is available, the breeder's efforts should be concentrated on building up a stock of sound, top-class individuals of similar type by efficient selection and line-breeding.

However, let it not be thought that in-breeding is beset with ominous overtones and represents a dire hazard for the breeder. Provided that the stock in use is good stock, sound, healthy and carrying within it no abnormal factors, breeding in this form can be carried on safely for many generations. There is one sure rule however, that must be followed. This is that every member of the resultant progeny which appears lacking in form, type and temperament, *must* be culled and quite ruthlessly. If this is not done, then in-breeding will not achieve any success, for you have to breed out the bad and mediocre and maintain the good. Remember, that the longer you maintain the defects or overlook them the greater time it will take to disperse them, if indeed this proves possible without the ruination of the strain. It should be noted that the closest form of in-breeding is by putting brother and sister together; father to daughter and mother to son coming lower down the line. The whole system of in-breeding is essentially a fascinating method of stock production, but frankly, it is strictly for the experts and not really for newcomers and beginners to the breed to embrace.

OUT-CROSSING

This is the mating of a pair of animals who are in no way related and have no common ancestors. The arrangement is normally made to introduce a desired attribute. The system may well achieve this, but just as easily it can bring in a number of other less wanted points taken from one or both parents. Generally, out-breeding produces an uneven litter and the good points aimed at in the progeny may well not appear in the mated pairs' first generation, often becoming apparent in the second generation, i.e. the grandchildren. Too many people are of the opinion that out-crossing, i.e. the introduction of new blood into an established strain, has the magical power of improving, invigorating, even producing something sensational in that strain. This is a fallacy – not only is it impossible for an out-cross to eliminate a fault in a single generation, but even faults hitherto unthought of could appear. This means that any dog used as an out-cross must be genetically pure with factors capable of correcting the in-bred fault which offends in the bitch. A dog capable of imparting correction which will more or less rectify the fault is a better out-cross proposition than the stud whose bloodlines permit him to more than swallow the fault and by so doing bring to the surface in the progeny some other undesirable feature, hitherto unnoted.

Selecting your stock

The prime aim of the novice breeder is to produce something good to prove himself in the world of Staffordshire Bull Terriers. It is easy enough to become deeply absorbed in dog breeding, especially if you are fortunate enough to achieve success in your early ventures in the game. First though, it is important and essential, to learn all about the breed. The Standard is the bible of the breed, which answers most questions. It has to be learned by the novice and applied by him to the living dog. Next, it is very necessary to get immersed in the breed and the only way to do this is to go to as many top shows as possible, shows where the best of Staffords are on show. Watch the judging and try and follow the judge's thoughts when he places the winning exhibits. Listen to the ringsiders' remarks and try and follow their reasoning too. Sometimes ringsiders talk a lot of sense, sometimes they do not, for they are not close-up on the exhibits and maybe they cannot see half what the judge can. The novice must not be backward in discussing the breed, its dogs, even its people with all and everyone who can help him with useful comment.

The top Staffordshire Bull Terrier kennels should be visited and the best dogs handled and got up close to – with their owners' permission, of course. Most breeders will be only too pleased to parade, even boast about their dogs and from such encounters much can be learnt. However, make sure the advice you get comes from the right people. There are people who have been in the breed a long time, but that does not make them experts, whereas there are experts who have been in the breed only a comparatively short time. Learn to sort out in the circle of enthusiasts those who talk sense, knowing what they are talking about. Remember at all times that most people with successful dogs have had to go through the mill to get where they are; to establish a sound, healthy and successful strain will have entailed much hard work, planning, financial outlay and quite a few disappointments and heartaches. Therefore, a word of thanks and appreciation is the order of the day for any knowledge gleaned from such friends.

As you get around the Stafford clan and inspect their dogs you will gradually develop and cultivate 'an eye' for a dog. This is essential, but not everyone manages to acquire this gift. A good 'eye' will save you a lot of money and help you to formulate sound decisions. It cannot be acquired in a few months, usually it comes after a year or two in the breed. Some folk need a lifetime to claim such an instinct. It will tell you what constitutes a good dog of a given type. Once you have the gift of recognising the right sort, you will find yourself able to pick out the right mating pair for your programme of breeding.

The old law of 'like begets like' is a sound one, although its veracity is sometimes debated. It develops from the system of appraisal normally used by successful livestock breeders when employing the breeding formula of visual appearance plus pedigree worth, already referred to. It *assumes* that when two parents of similar type are mated together their progeny will be of that type. Successful breeding by this method can be expected provided that it is supported by efficient line-breeding. This has to be based on a clear and true picture of the parents' ancestry as far back as possible. To achieve this, the mating pairs' pedigrees have to be studied so that each and every ancestor is pictured with its good and bad points. In effect, the pedigrees are made eloquent with the vital facts of the respective breed histories.

To follow the system through to a successful conclusion, you must find a mating pair which resemble each other structurally. They have to be good Staffordshire Bull Terriers in themselves, as near to the requirements of the breed Standard as possible, and certainly free from

Threapwood Nobleman of
Betchgreen, owned by Hans
and Edith Lachat.

Dorelu Red Sam, owned by
Mr and Mrs L. Lucy.

glaring faults. They have to be completely sound anatomically and
temperamentally and in first-class health. Never consider any animal

with vice or similar temperamental deficiency for any breeding pro-gramme and endeavour to ensure that the female family background can claim a series of good and reliable whelpers and bitches strong in their mothering qualities. With all such favourable points present, you will stand a very good chance of producing stock which conforms to the same good type.

When the puppies are bred, it will be found that the majority inherit many of the characteristics of both sire and dam, yet there will be some youngsters in the litter who do not bear much, if any, resemblance to either parent. Thus, if both parents have excellent heads, it is reasonable to expect that most of the progeny will have good heads, but it is quite likely that a few members of the litter will have indifferent heads. The cause of this feature could be that the individuals concerned are throw-backs to an early ancestor of whom you may not have much information, depending on whether you were able to complete with factual data the members of both parents' genealogical trees. On noting the apperance of youngsters with weak heads, you should be able to refer to your pedigree annotations and no doubt discover that the parental dam's grandam (for example only, please note) was commented upon for her weak head and skull. This could well mean that the dam of your puppies carries a tendency latently which she can transmit (has indeed transmitted in this instance) in subsequent generations.

When dissimilar types of Staffords are bred together, some puppies will tend to follow one parental type and some the other with possibly one or two falling midway between the two sorts. The latter kind, even if they prove worthwhile specimens, which would be unusual, will be of little use to someone with conscientious breeding in mind, for they will pass on to their own progeny the undesirable features of their own parents. Because of this danger alone, the value of knowing a lot about your dogs' pedigrees is apparent. The more you know of their ancestry the better your chances of successful breeding, provided this knowledge is applied intelligently and coupled with the determination to succeed in the drive to produce better Staffordshire Bull Terriers.

CHOOSING A BITCH

In any mating pair the female is of primary importance. The commonly recognised course of inheritance, when planning a union, is tail-male which considers objectively the sire, grand-sire, the great grand-sire and so on. In this way, the female lines are frequently overlooked, possibly because the task of setting out a breeding programme is made easier because the great number of offspring from a male enables the planner to assess better his worth as a sire; whereas the progeny from a bitch is, of course, limited. This preference for a male's influence is unfortunate, for tail-female course of inheritance is one of the most useful and important factors in breeding true to type. Without good bitches to breed to good dogs, no real or permanent advance towards perfection can ever be made.

It is important that the beginner should buy the best bitch he can afford, and this does not necessarily mean the most expensive. Today, there are highly competent and reputable Staffordshire Bull Terrier kennels specialising in show and breeding stock. A few discreet enquiries will quickly ascertain in which establishments the novice can place his faith. It must never be thought that a good bitch's conformation and points are of secondary importance. Certainly, it is important when breeding to select a good sire, but it is *vitally* important to have a good dam. Whereas with a good bitch one might breed some excellent stock with an ordinary stud dog, even the best of sires is hard put to it to produce something good out of a plain, perhaps nondescript, bitch. Good stock will never come readily from a poor female. Admittedly, there have been instances of mediocre dams producing the occasional big winner, but these exceptions are of little use to the breed generally for the poor bitch is a 'black mark' in the pedigree of any successful progeny she might conceive and which would be liable to throw back to her at a later date. Most breeders who produce what they believe to be a 'flyer' from sub-average background frequently congratulate themselves prematurely. Such advantages usually turn out to be only temporary.

Some guidance as to how a good bitch should be bought can be given.

Towstaff Rosabella, owned by Mr and Mrs R.S. Townsend.

Ch. Solo Gypsy Fiddler,
owned by Mr R. Wint.

Not many people can afford a Champion. Not every newcomer to the
breed would want to, anyway, and I am not too sure that it is a good
thing to try and take too short a cut to the top as a lot of the fun of the
game can be missed. It is better to buy an adult bitch or at least a well-
grown puppy – as free from faults in her make-up and type as possible.
Try and secure one with a pedigree which matches her good looks.
Remember the formula 'appearance plus pedigree' given in earlier pages
and you will know what to strive for in your purchase-to-be.

Study the living animal first; she *must* have a good head for this (as in
many breeds) is the dominant feature of the Staffordshire Bull Terrier. It
is the first part of the overall dog that anyone looks at, so it has to
impress and it must be good and correct. In effect, it has to be the main
feature of the well-balanced specimen. Take the head and skull in your
two hands and explore its contours. Do not be impressed overmuch with
exaggeration. A bitch should look feminine, so insist on a feminine head.
A masculine headpiece on a female would be a fault and would be
deplored by any competent judge of the breed. A doggy bitch is not quite
so bad as a bitchy dog, but both are detested in the breed and must be
avoided at all costs. Such a bitch might well produce coarse stock for you

and prove useless to any discerning breeder. The nobility of the headpiece should not need looking for as it should stand out at once. If it does not, then seek the reason why. It is possible that the cheeks bulge too much and fuse incorrectly with the muzzle. Maybe the muzzle itself is a shade too long or too shallow. Check eye emplacement, size and colour of the eyes, too. Eye colour can bear some relation to the colour of the coat, but a good dark eye is always better. Expression should be true; the bitch should not have a piercing, gimlet eye as that is more the look of a male. The expression, although sharply alert, should be feminine, as should everything else about her. Your understanding of the Staffordshire Bull Terrier breed Standard will be telling you what to seek in your purchase.

Ears, both size and set-on will need a check as will dentition and lips. The best ears are rose and small in form, neat and fairly thin in texture, supple to the touch and tidy. When folded back, the inner burr of the ear can be seen. You do not often see full drop and erect ears these days as they have been bred out. Semi-erect ears are still to be noted, the cause being due to some coarseness of the cartilage at the point where they join the skull, and this is an unwanted feature. Big ears are faulty and detract in general appearance to a large extent, so avoid any bitch so endowed. Small ears which fold back and are kept out of the way of a fighting adversary's jaws are ideal; conversely, big flaccid ears are soon grabbed hold of and represent a great disadvantage to their owner.

Go right over the body, starting down the neck over the shoulders and ribs back to the croup. Ensure a good symmetrical conformation; seek balance and angulation; and insist on a well-coupled animal. Some breeders aver that a bitch can be longer coupled than a dog. This may be true, but do not allow too much latitude in this concession, for in excess a lot will be lost in the bitch's balance and general appearance. Legs and feet are of great importance too. Any Stafford with poor feet could never express herself when moving, no matter how good she might be in other points; so move her away from you and towards you until you are satisfied she has good limbs and feet and knows how to use them to her (and your) advantage. Note that her legs should be straight and well-boned, set rather wide apart without looseness at the shoulders and showing no weakness at the pasterns at which point the feet turn out a little – so says the breed Standard on forequarters etc. It is necessary for the fore-legs to be set rather wide apart to allow ample chest development. Length of leg, if allowing too much daylight to show below the body, can throw the animal out of balance. Bone structure has its importance, the quality of the bone is best described by the word 'ample'. Heavy bone leans towards coarseness which is unwanted in a female. Light bone is a transmittable fault and if it exists in the bitch she is unlikely to be of much use to a serious breeder. Not only will she fail to give good effect if she is shown, but her offspring will either show similar weakness or carry the fault through to their own progeny. The old adage, 'What's bred in the bone will out in the flesh', infers that what has been passed down the female line over the generations will always show itself in subsequent generations.

The tail is another feature important to the true visual balance of a Stafford. The tail should be of medium length, low set and tapering to a point. It should also be carried rather low, not curling much and can be likened to an old-fashioned pump-handle. It is a distinctive tail and is important to her whole outline and refined appearance. A short tail gives a look of cloddiness, whereas a long tail lacks strength and detracts from a dog's balance, especially when viewed from the rear. The correct length is usually indicated in a tail which measures barely to the point of

Constones Ow'zatt, owned by Mr P. Snow.

hock. Tail carriage depends largely upon the angle or position of the sacrum in relation to the spine, the sacrum finishing where the root of the tail commences. It is essential that the pump-handle effect of the tail is there – it is typical of the Staffordshire and the root of the tail should be strong. A gay tail, i.e. one which is carried high and above the level of the back, proudly and curled, is an anathema and a bad fault. A low-set tail is bad too and is often found in dogs with a distinct falling-away at the croup. It is also very unsightly. Remember, some of the old sporting fraternity believed that a dog with an over-long, low-set tail was a coward, but such an opinion is unlikely to hold much credence.

Never be hurried into making an assessment or confirming your selection. If ,the owner of the bitch you are considering appears to be impatient or attempts to influence your choice with sales talk or unsolicited comment, best let the bitch go elsewhere. Any reputable kennel will understand your desire to ensure the purchase of a good bitch for your foundation; in fact, a breeder might well welcome the purchaser who wants to make up his or her own mind; at least it decides where the responsibility will rest.

Given ample time then, you can assess the Stafford bitch's character and temperament. If she seems cowed, she is no good at all, even though you may prove competent in reassuring her at a later date, for the damage has been done, usually irreparably. If she lacks verve and cheerfulness you might wish to know why. One does not want a Stafford which fusses over every stranger, but most of the Bull breeds are 'matey' to use an apt expression, and you can expect at least some friendliness and good nature to be expended upon you. See how alert she is, how watchful, how ready for a game. Is she well endowed with Staffordshire Bull Terrier type? The possession of this attribute especially is essential to an animal required for exhibition and breeding.

As advised earlier, a bitch's mothering capacity is important and this has been referred to in earlier pages. No one wants a dam who deserts or stamps on her young and may even carry this propensity to pass on to those of her progeny who procreate in turn. A few tactful enquiries as to these points might prove useful. On the other hand, if she is a maiden, then only time will tell you how she is geared to rear puppies. Should there be some doubt as to her ability at the task then avoid her at all costs, for a bad mother can be a worry as well as an expense.

It would seem superfluous to warn against purchasing a bitch with a faulty mouth. However, people still make purchases and pay large sums for new stock without making reasonably sure, at least, that their bitch (or dog for that matter) has every chance of finishing up with a level mouth. If buying an adult, as we have discussed, then a bitch of say a year old with her dentition complete and established, will surely reveal her mouth value once her mouth has been opened and inspected. Any variation from perfect needs thinking about. An indifferent mouth in an adult is unlikely to improve, more likely it will worsen as the months go by. It is by far the safer plan to ensure a good level jaw line in the first instance and trust that nothing will go wrong with it. The overshot and undershot jaws (faults in the breed Standard) are considered as very bad by most breed enthusiasts and judges, some of whom are often guilty of amplifying the severity of these faults ad infinitum. They are indeed hereditary, but in modern breeding a good deal of their influence has been eradicated.

BUYING A PUPPY

It is advisable when buying a puppy from a breeder to specify your needs, such as whether you require the Staffordshire Bull Terrier for exhibition or merely as a pet and companion. If it is the latter, then it is reasonable to suppose that the price will be rather lower than for a show prospect, for the pet puppy may well have some fault or deficiency which would preclude him from winning in competition. The reliable breeder will advise you and charge accordingly, but make sure that you go to someone who knows how to advise you.

Let us consider then the main points to look for when selecting a *good* Staffordshire Bull Terrier puppy of, say, two months old. Firstly, what are you going to buy – a dog or a bitch? In the author's opinion, a bitch is often preferable. Dogs are fine if you are fortunate enough to own a good one who evaluates himself to your advantage in the show-ring. Then people with bitches will want to use him at stud and with a number of bitches coming to him at regular intervals he will be happy and settle down to a smug sort of existence, even developing into a bit of a 'show-off', which will make him a good guard in the home and an active and probably pugnacious male out of doors. Such Staffordshire Bull Terriers are good to own, provided you feel young enough and active enough to manage them! But the deprived dog, i.e. the male that by virtue of his indifferent make and shape and unattractiveness to the breeder does not get used at stud, can prove an embarrassment and even a nuisance. When he gets to about ten months of age and the sexual urge is upon him, he will wish to seek a mate. His natural instinct will draw him out of doors and this means that he will wish to wander beyond the confines of your house and garden. Indoors, the deprived dog can commence to express his desires by 'working' on articles of furniture or furnishings or even upon the legs of members of the household. Such offensive manners cannot be tolerated and even with discipline applied to the animal, the pleasures of pedigree dog ownership are largely lost.

On the other hand, a bitch, should she not come up to expectations in show-ring potential, can always be the medium which will allow you to breed and probably produce the show-dog you desire. She has her natural awkward times of being on heat about three times every two years, but the Staffordshire Bull Terrier bitch is, generally speaking, a pretty clean creature at such periods and is usually not a nuisance. There exists, of course, the hazard of enquiring males, but the market can offer a variety of mating deterrents, most of them effective. Further, a bitch is often a better guard than a dog and she seems more loyal to her family. She is certainly less inclined to wander (apart from the time when she is ripe for mating) and as a 'nursemaid' to the children she is unequalled. A well-bred bitch puppy is an asset, without doubt. When you have the opportunity of buying one, take your time in making a thorough assessment and buy her between eight and twelve weeks if from the nest – the later the better in this period, for you will see more what you are getting.

Always try and see a litter intact, i.e. before any other person has had a chance to select from it. Next, see the lot of them on the move. You will see the five or six which comprise the average complement involved running free, either in their kennel or preferably on an open lawn. From the batch two or three will stay near you, two or three will vanish, either to get away from you or satisfy some curiosity. Take your time with the friendly ones; examine them on the ground while they are around your feet. Pick them up carefully; get the 'feel' of them. Make sure there is no prominent sternum (breastbone) pressing into your hand. Some might interpret this as indicative of a potentially deep chest or brisket, such as a well-made Stafford requires. It is not – it is just a plain case of pigeon-chest and a weak structural point. Feel the ribs; these should be rounded and firm. Look at the limbs; these should be well-boned, fairly substantial, rounded and no 'flute' formation, especially in the pastern (knee) region. The feet should be well-formed and not splayed in the toes. A puppy's feet will tighten up as he grows on, provided he is not run on soft ground, but the toes should not show wide gaps between the digits, even at this stage.

Open the mouth; this is an important examination because Staffordshire Bull Terriers having the old Bulldog as an ancestor are inclined to inherit that dog's tendency towards an undershot jaw formation. Thus, if the puppy's mouth is already undershot, i.e. with the lower row of front teeth (incisors) projecting beyond the upper set, it is fair to assume that it will carry this fault for the rest of its life. From your point of view the youngster will be of no use to you. Next, hold the puppy up to the light and inspect its jaw formation in profile. Some puppies, even those with teeth seemingly placed correctly, indicate by their jutting and pugnacious lower jaw formation that they will finish up undershot by the time they have assumed complete dentition.

Consider then the depth of the puppy's muzzle and the depth of skull. Both need to be deep and powerful, even at this early age. The fore-face should be short, too. Puppies of eight weeks with longish muzzles *always* make adults which are too long in muzzle. The head should be broad too. Take a look at the position of the eyes. If these are broadly spaced it is likely that the width of the animal's head will be of good width too for it is seldom that broadly spaced eyes are set in a narrow lean skull. Run both hands down from the skull to the muzzle, one hand on either side of the head. The feel should be of a solid, blocky and short mass, there being plenty of 'bump' where the cheeks will eventually develop a distinctly prominent bone formation.

Stand the puppy up sideways and look at it. It should look square, solid and blocky body-wise – just like a little cart-horse. In fact, it should seem to fit inside an imaginary square, giving an impression of substance and balance. Bring the puppy round, tail facing you. Run your finger and thumb down the tail. It should have a smooth run all the way down, no bunchy gristle mid-way, indicative of a tendency towards screw-tail. The tail should be fairly short, whip-like in appearance, but with ample thickness at the set-on. Good bone is shown at this point as it is on the limbs. Take heed of the hind-legs; they should be straight. If they appear cow-hocked at eight weeks, then it is clear that a lot of hard work and careful feeding will have to be put into the puppy to produce straight and parallel limbs at maturity.

Look closely at his front. He should have a good stolid formation aft, nice straight well-boned legs with the elbows tucked into the side and under the body, never pointing outwards. The adult Staffordshire Bull Terrier's feet are allowed to turn out a little at the pasterns, but with a very young eight-week-old puppy distinct evidence of this might indicate weakness at the pasterns, so place your preference on feet which run more or less in a straight line with the legs. Plenty of time for a Stafford to show that his feet turn out a little at the pasterns when he is a few months older. The front should be fairly wide, room enough for a smallish hand to be placed on the chest, under the brisket between the legs. It should feel muscled and solid. Put the puppy down and let it run and move around. Small puppies are often difficult to assess in movement as they leap and twist and climb, so get the breeder to call it away from you. He will run in a straight line, more or less, and you will quickly note any imperfections in his actions. Contrive to view him moving towards you to complete your assessment of his action and physical soundness.

Pick him up again, turn him over and examine his genitals. At eight weeks it is not always possible to determine whether a male is entire, i.e. with both testicles descended into the scrotum. However, it may be possible and if assured on this point, all is well. If it cannot be determined then you take a chance if you accept the puppy. However, in about eight cases out of ten your chances are that he will be entire. Ears are difficult to assess in young puppies. Sometimes tiny, thin tissue ears, with thick cartilage where they join the skull, turn out semi-erect or even erect ears with maturity. Erect ears you *must* avoid getting, and even semi-erect, although conceded by the breed Standard and liked by some fanciers, are secondary to rose ears, which fold back, exposing the inner burr. Run the fingers gently over the ears from skull juncture to tip. Small ears, with malleable tissue at their base stand a good chance of shaping up well and as required, but much can be learnt about the future of a youngster's ears by examining his parents, if they are around to see. Ear type is transmitted freely and if, on examination, you approve a puppy's ears and later satisfy yourself as to the parents' ears, then you are usually on quite safe ground.

Given satisfaction on all the points discussed, you should stand a very good chance of rearing a typical adult, but remember that your chances of picking a champion are quite slim. It is assumed that in your process of selecting a puppy you will have examined him carefully to establish his good condition. Your eye will tell you a great deal – a puppy in sparkling good condition, well covered with flesh, a glossy coat and bright eyes stands out as in good trim. A coat which 'stares', i.e. with rough up-sticking tufts might indicate worms or too economic rearing. Such condition could well be improved upon with individual attention such as you would arrange for him. Check around the genitals; the region should be free from rashes, spots and other signs of discomfort. Lift up his tail for signs of soreness and run a finger from set-on of tail along the spine, turning the hair of his coat back to establish the fact that no parasites are present. If the puppy has a bump on its navel, question it with the breeder. This is probably an umbilical hernia – in effect a rupture. It often happens to first-borns and from a maiden bitch, who has been agitated or anxious in producing her first puppy at her initial whelping. Avoid a puppy with this protuberance if you can. It is unsightly, to say the least, but small ones seldom constitute a true unsoundness and either diminish as the animal grows on or can be disposed of by simple surgery.

The foregoing factors apply, as has been said, to selecting a puppy of around eight weeks of age. For the person who is anxious to strengthen his chances of owning a show specimen, then his choice will have to be from older, more mature puppies. It has been said that one can do this with reasonable success from youngsters of around five months old. It is true that a puppy of this age is often looking worse than it will do at any age of its life and if you can find a handsome five-monther then your chances of owning a beautiful adult are quite good. However, the cost will probably be more – such a puppy, if his owner knows the breed, will almost certainly cost a lot. On the other hand, he may be a confirmed faddist for some particular point in the breed which he feels his puppy does not or will not possess, and be ready to dispose of the youngster for a reasonable sum. This need not deter you from buying the puppy if *you* like it. Many experienced breeders have been known to run on for several weeks a couple of promising puppies from a considered show litter, believing that they would hit the jackpot with one of them, only to sell the 'flyer' and keep the mediocre one for themselves by mistake.

Whatever the age of the puppy you buy, always check with the seller as to the type of feeding it has been used to.

Mr R. W. Harper's Ch. Pitmax the Matador.

CHOOSING THE SIRE

It should not be thought that the wins attributed to a stud dog necessarily make him a good sire. A lot of breeders are influenced by a dog's show wins, which may well not be of much value when properly assessed. It is not unusual for a dog to win his title in quite mediocre competition or at shows which are unpopular with exhibitors generally and are sparsely attended. Such shows could be located in inconvenient geographical venues or rendered unpalatable to an exhibitor owing to a bad classification or promotion. For such reasons it is important for the bitch owner who seeks a stud for his charge to attend as many big shows as he can. There he should find the best of Staffordshire Bull Terriers doing the show circuit in the current year and then he can assess the worth of every win for himself.

Ch. Bodjer of Kenstaff, owned by Mr and Mrs I.C. Gough.

A stud dog should be chosen solely for the value of his progeny, rather than for the number of first prizes he has won. It is only by employing the former rule that you will become a successful breeder. You may have a good bitch but she will have some fault; the perfect one has yet to be bred and it is essential for your own success that you make yourself aware of any failings. If you are blind to these faults or refuse to accept their presence then you might be well-advised to give up the idea of pedigree dog breeding forthwith. Only a man who knows the weaknesses in his Stafford can have any hope of correcting them. It is possible to breed out any deficiency with care and calculation over a number of generations, according to the intensity of the fault and the time available, but the planning to achieve good results without introducing faults, hitherto non-existent, is the work of a dedicated breeder.

Some misinformed breeders think the way to correct a fault is to utilise a stud dog endowed with the exact opposite of that fault. For example, suppose your bitch is too short in the back and body, the mistaken theory is that she should be mated to a dog who is extra long in the back, the belief being that one extreme will cancel out the other. In fact, this is no more than mating fault to fault and will do little more than produce accentuated faults. It is feasible that an odd puppy or two will crop up falling midway between the two parental types, but the main result of the litter would be to produce some puppies which were too long in the back (resembling their sire) and some which were too short in the back (resembling their dam). Worst of all, the whole litter, however they finished up, would represent indifferent breeding potential when their time came to reproduce, for they would carry the tendency to transmit both parent's inherent faults to their progeny. The secret in breeding is to find a stud dog for the bitch who is the correct length in his back, then, as has been shown, some puppies would tend to be correct in their length of back – not only that, but they would carry the power to transmit only one fault, i.e. overlong backs, rather than two. It will be realised that this illustrates only one example, but numerous examples could be given by applying any pair of opposite faulty characteristics, for instance tallness and shortness of leg, apple heads and lean heads, loose shoulders and Terrier fronts and so on.

Mating

It is unwise to mate a bitch at her first heat, normally expected to occur when a Staffordshire Bull Terrier female is around eight months of age. Some bitches start off their seasons earlier, some later. Apart from the fact that it is rather unfair to put maternal duties upon a puppy at her initial heat, there is also a distinct chance of her 'missing' and also one of possible whelping complications. This might apply especially in the case of an immature specimen. Many breeders favour the second heat for first time mating and this tenet would normally point to a bitch of say, fourteen to fifteen months when she would be in a ripe yearling stage and able to embrace the sometimes onerous duties of motherhood in her stride. Thereafter, it is possible, provided she whelped well, to mate her again the following heat, this being a pattern generally accepted as sound procedure by most experienced breeders. Following this, it is humane and wise to allow one heat to pass between each mating for this will give her a chance of building up her body meanwhile.

When planning a mating and having decided which stud dog to use with the bitch, a provisional booking should be made with his owner. This advice can be confirmed as soon as the bitch begins to show 'colour' when a definite date, about twelve days ahead, can be determined. As is commonly known, a bitch's period of season (or *oestrum*) is between sixteen and twenty-one days. No definite time can be given for mating a bitch, as individuals vary, often quite considerably. The best time, usually, is when the coloured discharge from the vagina has ceased for a day or two. Some bitches will be found quite ready to receive a dog at any time between the tenth and fifteenth day, but others have to be caught at a certain time, often experiencing just a few hours of ripeness around the middle of their season. If a bitch is this way disposed, then special arrangements will need to be made. The best plan is to kennel her near to the selected stud dog during her vital period so that she can be introduced to him immediately she shows willing. Frankly, such bitches are a nuisance, but if she is a good one and the chances of producing something good from her exist, then it can be worth considering a little extra expense and trouble. Most bitches are ready for union on their twelfth or thirteenth day.

It is normal procedure to take bitch to dog. If the stud dog resides a long way off, then you may have to send her to him by rail box. It is best, however, to arrange to take her yourself if possible. Not only do you save your bitch consternation and distress at a critical period, but you can also be sure that the mating is a success with the stud dog of your choice. Further, the bitch is far more likely to settle down to a mating if you are standing by her. Bitches bustled alone into an unknown house or kennel with strange humans and a bombastic stud dog, then pushed off home in an uncomfortable box, often 'miss' and then all the time and expense entailed has been wasted and there is another six months to wait before you can try her again.

The best time for mating is early morning, both dog and bitch having had ample opportunity to run around first and empty themselves prior to the union. Neither animal should have been fed for at least twelve hours previously. If your bitch is a maiden and the stud dog you have chosen for her is experienced, then everything will probably go well for the dog will normally conduct matters efficiently.

However, if the dog is an untried one, some care will have to be taken. He will probably rush about all over the place in excited anticipation, act stupidly and put the bitch so ill at ease that she will either attack him or refuse completely to co-operate with him when finally he calms down. With such a mating, at least two handlers should be present, one of whom ought to have had some experience of dog-mating procedure. The bitch's owner should hold her collar firmly and the best way to do this is to put the thumbs under her collar on either side of her head. The rest of the hands can then take in her ears and the inside of the wrists can be used against her cheeks to steady her head and prevent it jerking round to savage the dog as he mounts her. Some people muzzle a difficult bitch with a conventional muzzle or tape and bandage at such a time, but this is rather drastic and should be avoided if possible. Not only does it border on cruelty, but even the wickedest bitches appear affected adversely by forced matings. Assuming that the bitch's head is being held comfortably and she is accepting this with reasonably good grace, the second handler should support her rear end by putting his hand beneath her loins. The dog can then be encouraged to mount her if he is inexperienced and it may be necessary to give him some manipulative treatment and assistance by guiding him into the bitch's vulva. For those with young up-and-coming stud dogs, this is an important training right from the start of their affairs. In difficult cases especially, a handler's aid and co-operation is appreciated, indeed expected, by the trained stud dog. The author had a dog so well trained (or so usefully disposed) that he refused to do anything except the sexual act itself! The bitch would arrive and stand there or commence to show off when he entered, expecting him to rush her. Instead, he would glance idly at her, look up at his handler and wait for the bitch to be placed rear end on to him. He would then mount her at once and the whole thing would be over in no time. He had well over a hundred matings – hardly any of which were 'misses' and these were usually attributed to the bitches.

A 'natural' mating is recommended by some breeders. This entails leaving the stud dog and the bitch in season both to their own devices. It is hoped that they will effect copulation without any outside assistance. This is all very well if it works out satisfactorily, but often such natural matings are seldom effected without some distress being caused to one of the animals. For this reason alone a supervised union is better. Pedigree Staffordshire Bull Terriers have a high monetary value these days and, tough though they may be, there seems little sense in letting two strong, powerful and determined animals alone in a run or paddock and returning later to find slit ears, gashed eyes or at worst a ruptured stud dog. Calamities like this can occur easily enough, even between a couple who normally run amicably together.

The dog's natural instinct will cause him to take the initiative in the mating and once he has entered the bitch he should be held there for a few moments, both animals being steadied until a 'tie' has been effected. This will indicate conclusively that seminal fluid is being deposited. The tie, although not essential, is always a very satisfactory state to witness when mating dogs; it lasts usually between fifteen and thirty minutes. During this time the two animals will probably have brought themselves round tail-to-tail, the accepted position for mating dogs. Should they seem to be struggling to get round to achieve this formation, the handlers should assist them. One should hold the bitch's head, the other gently swivel the dog round, lifting one of his hind legs up and over the bitch's back. Keep on swivelling his head round and the lifted leg will follow round too and eventually come down to the ground. Both animals will then be perfectly comfortable and can continue so placed. In order that the bitch should not march forward dragging the dog backwards behind her while the union is taking effect, the pair are best watched until the dog disengages. He should then be removed from her presence and left in a quiet room or abode to regain his composure. His personal comfort can be attended to, if necessary, by ensuring that the sheath covering the penis has been returned to its natural position. Both animals should be watered and rested after adequate feeding. One service is usually sufficient from a dog regularly at stud. An untried dog, having his first successful mating could be allowed another within thirty-six hours of the first, if one's convenience allows. It may be that the first service will have done nothing but stimulate the second, hence this precaution.

Some explanation as to the workings of a 'tie' might be in order in this section. It occurs when a dog is at his highest rate of sexual excitement, i.e. when he has entered the bitch to the extent of his final thrust and is pumping something like several million sperm into her. At this stage the penis will have undergone some change. It will have swollen to three or four times its normal size and the bulb, which is a rather hard swelling not unlike the size and shape of a ping-pong ball, situated half way along the length of the penis, will hold the pair together, 'tied' in effect until that bulb deflates when the union concludes. Some people wonder why dog and bitch come tail-to-tail when mating. It is believed that the position taken is some provision of Nature for a mating pair in the wild state. A dog and bitch so occupied and placed in this way have a biting armament at both ends; not only this, but they can travel their armament in a complete circle. Thus, any attacker at such an inconvenient time can be reasonably well withstood and the pair are far less vulnerable than if their joint backs were turned against any onslaught.

It might be of interest to some that artificial insemination is available to the canine world as indeed it is to humans. In this process, living semen (the fluid containing the spermatozoa) is drawn off from the stud dog then passed by artificial means into the vaginal passage of the bitch at the time of her oestral peak. It is necessary to obtain Kennel Club permission to do this in order that any progeny from a mating by artificial insemination can be exhibited. This rule applies to Kennel Clubs in all countries and a certificate from a competent and qualified veterinary surgeon to the effect that the work has been carried out properly would be required. The system has its advantages in that semen contained in special vials can'be flown by air to bitches resident in other lands, allowing them the privilege of acquiring the services of noted stud dogs abroad without the irritations and expense of quarantine restrictions and import licences.

The bitch in whelp

Many breeders prefer to worm their bitches prior to a mating. This cannot be a bad idea and the breeder should then administer a reliable vermifuge or veterinarily recommended medicine not later than one week after the end of her season. The normal period of gestation is sixty-three days, although deliveries before or after the date anticipated are by no means uncommon. Such extended periods may be as much as a tardy five days. Early puppies might arrive forward at a similar period and these would be sound and healthy, no doubt, but probably just that period lacking in maturity – in effect, just a little backward. However, this should occasion no worry for they will speedily pick up lost ground. In early litters of this kind it is quite likely that instead of the eyes opening on the tenth day, as usual, they will not open until the thirteenth or fourteenth day. Early litters sometimes occur with bitches whelping for the first time.

Exercise of the bitch in whelp should be normal up to within a

TABLE SHOWING WHEN A BITCH IS DUE TO WHELP

Served Jan. Whelps March	Served Feb. Whelps April	Served March Whelps May	Served April Whelps June	Served May Whelps July	Served June Whelps Aug.	Served July Whelps Sept.	Served Aug. Whelps Oct.	Served Sept. Whelps Nov.	Served Oct. Whelps Dec.	Served Nov. Whelps Jan.	Served Dec. Whelps Feb.
1 5	1 5	1 3	1 3	1 3	1 3	1 2	1 3	1 3	1 3	1 3	1 2
2 6	2 6	2 4	2 4	2 4	2 4	2 3	2 4	2 4	2 4	2 4	2 3
3 7	3 7	3 5	3 5	3 5	3 5	3 4	3 5	3 5	3 5	3 5	3 4
4 8	4 8	4 6	4 6	4 6	4 6	4 5	4 6	4 6	4 6	4 6	4 5
5 9	5 9	5 7	5 7	5 7	5 7	5 6	5 7	5 7	5 7	5 7	5 6
6 10	6 10	6 8	6 8	6 8	6 8	6 7	6 8	6 8	6 8	6 8	6 7
7 11	7 11	7 9	7 9	7 9	7 9	7 8	7 9	7 9	7 9	7 9	7 8
8 12	8 12	8 10	8 10	8 10	8 10	8 9	8 10	8 10	8 10	8 10	8 9
9 13	9 13	9 11	9 11	9 11	9 11	9 10	9 11	9 11	9 11	9 11	9 10
10 14	10 14	10 12	10 12	10 12	10 12	10 11	10 12	10 12	10 12	10 12	10 11
11 15	11 15	11 13	11 13	11 13	11 13	11 12	11 13	11 13	11 13	11 13	11 12
12 16	12 16	12 14	12 14	12 14	12 14	12 13	12 14	12 14	12 14	12 14	12 13
13 17	13 17	13 15	13 15	13 15	13 15	13 14	13 15	13 15	13 15	13 15	13 14
14 18	14 18	14 16	14 16	14 16	14 16	14 15	14 16	14 16	14 16	14 16	14 15
15 19	15 19	15 17	15 17	15 17	15 17	15 16	15 17	15 17	15 17	15 17	15 16
16 20	16 20	16 18	16 18	16 18	16 18	16 17	16 18	16 18	16 18	16 18	16 17
17 21	17 21	17 19	17 19	17 19	17 19	17 18	17 19	17 19	17 19	17 19	17 18
18 22	18 22	18 20	18 20	18 20	18 20	18 19	18 20	18 20	18 20	18 20	18 19
19 23	19 23	19 21	19 21	19 21	19 21	19 20	19 21	19 21	19 21	19 21	19 20
20 24	20 24	20 22	20 22	20 22	20 22	20 21	20 22	20 22	20 22	20 22	20 21
21 25	21 25	21 23	21 23	21 23	21 23	21 22	21 23	21 23	21 23	21 23	21 22
22 26	22 26	22 24	22 24	22 24	22 24	22 23	22 24	22 24	22 24	22 24	22 23
23 27	23 27	23 25	23 25	23 25	23 25	23 24	23 25	23 25	23 25	23 25	23 24
24 28	24 28	24 26	24 26	24 26	24 26	24 25	24 26	24 26	24 26	24 26	24 25
25 29	25 29	25 27	25 27	25 27	25 27	25 26	25 27	25 27	25 27	25 27	25 26
26 30	26 30	26 28	26 28	26 28	26 28	26 27	26 28	26 28	26 28	26 28	26 27
27 31	27 1	27 29	27 29	27 29	27 29	27 28	27 29	27 29	27 29	27 29	27 28
28 1	28 2	28 30	28 30	28 30	28 30	28 29	28 30	28 30	28 30	28 30	28 1
29 2	29 3	29 31	29 1	29 31	29 31	29 30	29 31	29 1	29 31	29 31	29 2
30 3		30 1	30 2	30 1	30 1	30 1	30 1	30 2	30 1	30 1	30 3
31 4		31 2		31 2		31 2	31 2		31 2		31 4

fortnight of the big day when the puppies are expected. After this time the walks should be easier and perhaps slower. Such things as jumping and rough play should be discouraged and her feeding should be such as to maintain her good condition and allow enough extra nourishment (including calcium phosphate sources) to help with the development in the puppies to come. It has been found useful with a bitch shortly to whelp to give a small teaspoonful of medicinal paraffin every day. This will keep her bowels open and oil her up nicely inside. This course is a short one and need not commence much before ten days prior to her expected whelping date. Just before the date of her whelping her food should be reduced a little and the feeds should be staggered. There is no reason to envisage any difficulties arising with the whelping, especially if the birth is from a sound, acknowledged good whelping family of bitches. However, it is always a good thing to be prepared for the occasional situation which might cause some awkward moments and be forewarned by being forearmed with the remedies.

A WHELPING BOX

Make sure you have a good whelping box ready for the bitch to nest in. If you do not then she is quite capable of making her own selection of a suitable place for her puppies to settle in. This might be in the centre of the bed in the master bedroom, underneath the sideboard or below a rose-bush at the far end of your garden, in fact any place likely to prove difficult from ousting her once whelping had started!

The whelping box shown in the accompanying sketch (Fig. 15) will give some idea as to what should be made ready. A sort of 'pig-rail'

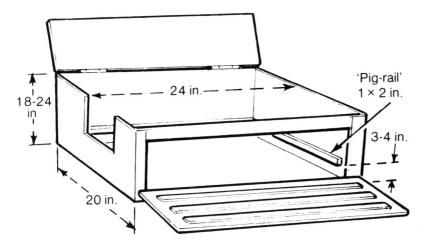

FIG. 15 Whelping box.

should be screwed in round the inner sides, this being a valuable adjunct, the idea having prevented many whelps being squashed by clumsy mothers. The rail itself should allow ample room for the puppy to rest under its shelf-like protection with the bitch leaning against it. The lid, when closed, makes a raised platform for the bitch to jump upon and put herself at rest out of her youngsters' way when she wishes to avoid their attentions during the later weaning period. The drop-front of the box which is ribbed with slats will permit the breeder to control the comings and goings of the puppies when they are at walking stage. The overall measurements can be adapted to the girth of the bitch, but 60cm (24in) across 50cm (20in) deep and 45–50cm (18–20in) high seems a reasonable size for such a box. The 'pig-rail' made out of wood 2.5 x 5cm (1 x 2in) should stand about 7.5–10cm (3–4in) up from the base of the box. This then is a general idea for a whelping box and the breeder who is a useful hand at woodwork will be able to modify and improvise on this to suit his own ideas. In the matter of bedding, if any, absolute hygiene must be observed. Personally, I would not use any bedding, but some people like to use sheets of newsprint during the whelping which can be speedily exchanged as they get soiled; others like a disinfected piece of hessian or crash material. This must be nailed securely to the base of the box with strong flat-headed nails which cannot be dislodged when the bitch begins to scratch. Avoid at all costs deep layers of hay or straw under which whelps could snuggle and be smothered. The same danger exists with the use of blankets and soft linings.

Introduce the bitch to her new quarters a good week before the event. By the time she whelps she will have become used to her new surroundings away from the family circle and be ready to commence her maternal duties without any distractions. Her temperature when about to whelp will usually drop below 37.7°C (100°F), even to 36.4°C (97.5°F). This should be a fair indication to the breeder that labour pains are imminent. The bitch will probably refuse food and drink at this stage and show some agitation in preparing her nest, scratching and swivelling around on herself in typical pre-whelping fashion. Just before she whelps she may well relax into a profound sleep, this being Nature's way of preparing her for the onerous period ahead.

STARTING TO WHELP

The cautious breeder will have prepared himself for the whelping, firstly by having warned his local veterinary surgeon of the event in advance and asked him to come out should complications ensue. Secondly, he will have provided himself with a good emergency or first-aid kit. The contents of this will be according to his personal experience with a whelping, but for the newcomer to the exercise, a good guide would be:

1. Packet of fairly large disposable tissues.
2. Sharp sterilised scissors. Probe-end surgical type is best.
3. Pre-cut lengths, about 18cm (7in), surgical thread or strong cotton.
4. Vaseline and a liquid antiseptic as free from strong aroma as possible.
5. Clean towel for drying hands, and pieces of clean towelling.
6. Well-scoured clean basin and a covered stone hot-water bottle.
7. Emergency feeding bottle.
8. Quantity of brandy, which if required should be doled out *very* sparingly, i.e. drop or two at a time in a teaspoon.
9. A Thermos flask containing warm milk and a saucer bowl.

When the bitch is about to whelp she will evince a slight straining or rippling along her back. These are muscles reflexing and it may not be repeated immediately, but will come on more frequently and the straining more apparent until there are three or four strains at intervals of about the same number of minutes. Probably at this time, the first warm milk drink should be given to the bitch to hasten progress, but very often best results are achieved by leaving her alone. If however, the animal is already very late in producing her puppies and the breeder is experiencing some real anxiety as to her welfare then it will be wise to call in the veterinary surgeon without delay.

Puppies are born one by one and are presented head first, this being the normal delivery. However, those that come rear end first need occasion no alarm unless the dam seems distressed in which case she may need assistance. Rear-end first birth is known as 'breech' birth and can prove awkward although not necessarily. A more serious aspect of this kind of birth lies with the brachycephalic breeds, such as Pekinese, Pugs, etc. i.e. members of the large-headed, flat-faced families with small pubic apertures. Every birth has to be assessed on its merits or demerits. This is when a breeder's experience will tell him what action to take. Any form of interference during whelping is undesirable and it is best always to let Nature take its course. Only when it is sensible to assume that the situation looks critical should veterinary help be employed.

Maiden bitches sometimes need special attention. Occasionally, a maiden will panic at the sight of her first puppy, or be distraught at her labour pains, hitherto unexperienced. Sometimes a bitch will make no effort to produce her puppies and will lie dormant when the first puppy appears at her rear end. Should this happen, the breeder must take up one of the pieces of clean towelling he has standing by and grip the newborn gently, easing it out of the dam in rhythm with the strains. The puppies appear each in its own liquid-filled sac. The experienced bitch

A fine litter by Textrix King Oberon out of Ch. Wardrum Dixie Queen, bred by Mr D. W. Smart.

will break the sac herself and this must be done in any case to allow the youngster to inhale air into its lungs. Failure to do this will cause the puppy to expire. The bitch should at once buffet the puppy with her tongue, applying what is really a form of artificial respiration. If she does not do this, the breeder must apply some firm massaging to its body. The bitch will then start to clean up the whelp with vigorous licking and this will remove unwanted slime and mucus around its mouth. The dam should also nip the umbilical cord which connects the whelp to the placenta or afterbirth which at this stage will still be inside her. If she does not appear to be expelling the placenta, the *cord* should be taken between finger and thumb and gently pulled to withdraw the afterbirth. Do not pull from the direction of the puppy itself. Any tug away from the youngster's navel may well cause an umbilical hernia, which apart from being a disfigurement in later life might necessitate a minor operation to disperse it. Tie a piece of your thread (surgical type is best) or strong cotton about 1.25cm (½in) away from the puppy's navel. Cut the umbilical cord at a short point 3.15cm (1½in) *above* the tie with your sterilised scissors or with a well-scrubbed finger and thumb. The placenta then should be disposed of, although some bitches eat this, it being an instinctive action which some animals inherited from the wild state, to give her sustenance. Temporarily incapacitated at such a time she would be unlikely to obtain food for twenty-four hours until able to leave her whelps and get food for herself. However, assuming she has not disposed the placentae, it is rather important for the domestic breeder to keep a count on the number of these as they are expelled. Once whelping is over they should be checked and their total made to correspond with the number of puppies born. Should it be apparent that a placenta has been retained by the bitch in her womb, then it will be advisable to call the veterinary surgeon who will expel it effectively with a suitable injection. By so doing it will probably save the bitch from a septic womb infection, not uncommon in cases of the retention of after-births.

Providing the pattern of whelping follows this form there is little to worry about. Between deliveries of her puppies the bitch will probably have short sleeps, then wake up, start straining again, and so on. Should she suddenly appear to slacken her efforts and the straining become noticeably weaker while it is obvious that some puppies remain in her, this could mean uterine inertia necessitating a Caesarian operation (see p. 97); but Staffordshire Bull Terriers are not particularly prone to such things and providing the bitch is well made, healthy and comes from a good whelping bitch family, no such situation should arise.

After whelping

Once it has been noted that the bitch has calmed down and is spending a lot of time cleaning herself, it is fairly obvious then that she has delivered her final puppy and whelping is complete. Her whole attitude will at once become entirely more relaxed. Let her have a drink of warm milk to which a little water has been added and a teaspoonful of glucose or a dessertspoonful of honey. If she can be persuaded to leave the whelping box and the brood to go outside and relieve herself, it will give you a chance to arrange a speedy clean-up, anything having been used for bedding disposed of and the puppies inspected to determine their sexes and to check that no abnormalities are present. Whelps with deformities, cleft palates etc. are better disposed of humanely at this time.

As soon as the bitch scurries back to her nest, suckling will commence and she should be left alone once it becomes clear that she is in control of the situation. It is better to darken the room a little and ensure that no strangers or other animals are allowed near her. Children should not be permitted to interfere with or handle the puppies and this rule should be adhered to for a few days, at least. She will need a lot of sleep at this time for she will be exhausted by her earlier efforts. Some breeders arrange with their veterinary surgeon to inject the dam at this time with penicillin. This contributes to inner cleanliness and gives some peace of mind in that no infection will develop as a result of the whelping and consequent lowering of the bitch's resistance.

The ideal litter will number five to six. Five is possibly better for these will thrive remarkably well on the average milk supply, whereas bigger litters not only absorb more and therefore lower the dam's constitution, but are slower to develop. Close attention must be given to any members of the litter who seem weaker to ensure that they are not ousted from the main inguinal teats which lie towards the groin area. If the litter has proved an extra large one and it is felt that the bitch cannot cope properly with it, or looks like being an indifferent mother, then a foster parent may have to be considered. Some bitches do not produce their milk very quickly and with the puppies screaming for food and nothing coming out, both dam and owner often become distressed. A veterinary surgeon will be able to deal with the hastening of milk flow, but if there seems a wide divergence between the number of puppies and the amount of milk forthcoming then it may be clear that a foster mother should be brought to the scene. The canine weekly journals usually indicate where these can be obtained and certain kennels specialise in their supply and are noted for clean and reliable bitches. The Collie breeds are particularly well-endowed with milk and make good fosters, but whether pure-bred or mongrels, their breeding is unimportant so long as ample milk is flowing to rear the Stafford puppies who will have to depend on their new mother. The foster mother should be introduced to the surplus puppies or the entire litter, as the case may be, as quickly as possible after the whelping.

The usual procedure of kennels which specialise in these foster parents is to use a bitch, frequently of doubtful origin, allow her to produce puppies, then dispose of them as soon as there is a call on her services from a person or kennel with a pedigree litter which has been rejected by its mother, or for some other breeding problem. Quite apart from the distress which is occasioned upon the foster parent bitch by having her own puppies removed from her and she herself being consigned on possibly a long trip in a small box to a strange and distant home, the danger exists that she may bring in some infection to the pedigree litter. The business of acquiring and using a foster mother is expensive in itself; if she brings in some disease that kills off the pedigree litter then she is worse than expensive, although it is no fault of her own, poor creature. Any breeder envisaging the use of a foster parent should ensure that its health and antecedents have been checked and approved by a qualified veterinary surgeon in her own locality first.

Dew claws

All puppies are born with these rudimentary digits (somewhat equivalent to the thumb in humans) on their forelegs; sometimes they appear on the hindlegs, but these latter are quite objectionable and no breeder proud of his stock likes to find them. The hind-leg dew claws, if any, must be removed immediately and a suitable time is when the puppies are four days old. The front leg dew claws in a Stafford are usually left on, most breeders viewing them as a traditional part-and-parcel of the breed. There is seldom any disadvantage in them, although occasionally they get mixed up with some obstruction and sustain rips and tears. The veterinary surgeon will soon dispose of any unwanted appendages, but a competent layman can do the job himself using a pair of sterilised snub-nosed scissors, cutting very close to the limb, stemming superfluous bleeding with an application of Friars Balsam or similar ointment. As with all minor operations of this type, careful watch must be kept on the wounds until they have healed. Such checks should be made twice daily.

Feeding the dam

For at least a day the bitch should have nothing but nourishing milk drinks. There are some excellent sustained milk foods on the market and these are ideal for the purpose. Frequency of feeding is usually about five times a day but, of course, the manufacturer's suggestions must be followed. A little raw meat can follow, providing her temperature is normal, but once it fluctuates then back to milk foods she should go. A recommended diet for the nursing bitch would be:

    7 am   Sustained milk drink of a proprietary make.
    10 am Meat (raw) chopped small.
    1 pm   Scrambled or poached egg with wheatmeal bread.
    4 pm   Milk food as at 7 am.
    7 pm   Raw meat again or carefully boned boiled fish.
    10 pm Milk food as at 7 am and 4 pm.

The quantity and distribution of the bitch's meals will depend largely on the size of her litter. The purpose of the feeding is not only to satisfy her, but to charge her with goodness which she can pass down to her puppies in the form of milk. A bitch with a full complement of puppies will obviously need proportionately more food than one with just two or three youngsters to feed. If she is nursing a biggish litter of say eight, then it might be advisable to give her an extra drink in the early hours for a few days following the whelping. Her own milk supply will be best built up with cold water and raw meat – these are best producers for milk quantity and quality – but if diarrhoea is noted, and this is common enough in a bitch after whelping, cut down on the volume of milk and give more water. It is also advisable to reduce her meat intake too for the time being until the condition has eased off.

After-whelping problems

ECLAMPSIA

It is not uncommon to find a bitch very excitable after she has whelped.

She will whine and give every indication of nervous distress and panting and may transport her puppies in her mouth from here to there without any apparent reason. The breeder's first action should be to confine her to a darkened room and give her as much reassurance and sympathetic attention as possible. The condition is known as Eclampsia and is a common enough condition in nursing bitches caused by a sudden deficiency of calcium in the blood, due to the heavy demand placed upon their reserves by having to produce large quantities of milk. It is usually the mature bitch which suffers from this condition rather than one with her first litter, although those with extra large litters can be affected. The initial symptoms are a change in expression, the bitch giving the impression of being dazed and uncertain of herself with staggering and some twitching in the front limbs. Panting and general distress are normal symptoms and your veterinary surgeon will probably inject with a preparation strong in calcium and phosphorus combined with Vitamin D to counteract the calcium deficiencies and curb the excitability. Relief is usually seen within a few minutes and after about half-an-hour the bitch will be back to normal.

If possible, give her a rest away from her puppies, but she may refuse to co-operate with you in this. In many cases, it is advisable to give the puppies supplementary feeds of such as 'Lactol', according to the directions for their size and age. The bitch may require at your veterinary surgeon's discretion a further injection later in the day, but in any case, she should be kept under constant supervision. The supplementary feeding given to the puppies will help to ease the drawing away of the calcium from their mother. Some breeders theorise that Eclampsia could be prevented in many cases if the bitch is progressively removed from her puppies for longer and longer periods each day. This would possibly be three or four minutes on the third day and increasing every day until at a month the bitch would be away for periods of several hours at a time over the day. These periods away from the puppies should be accompanied by exercise in the fresh air, running after a ball, etc. Most breeders will almost certainly follow this procedure to a greater or lesser degree in any case. But equally the bitch should never be forced to stay away from her puppies if this seems to upset her. The very fact of her becoming upset and anxious could well bring on an attack of Eclampsia, so her feelings have to be considered important at such a time. If any attack of Eclampsia seems imminent — for instance, if the bitch begins to pant suddenly and without apparent reason, whimpers, scratches in corners or tries to carry a puppy around in her mouth — then she will need further treatment until she is calm. There are suitable preparations on the market which deal adequately and well with this condition and one should be kept ready to use if needed, but the size of the dose should be prescribed by your veterinary surgeon. Such elixirs as

'Collo-Cal-D' are noted for their usefulness in the treatment of Eclampsia.

EXCESS MILK

Sometimes a whelping mother has too much milk, the surplus not being taken up quickly enough by her puppies, and congestion ensues with the milk exuding and caking over the breasts. The breasts most usually affected are the inguinals, i.e. the large ones at the rear. These become over-gorged with milk, inflamed and cause the dam a great deal of discomfort. In her irritation she will gnaw at them and in an advanced state abscesses will occur. To offset this, if you have a bitch showing signs of excess milk, relieve her condition by gently milking the nipples, and cut down her fluid supply at once. The only danger involved in dispersing a bitch's milk in this way is that it encourages more to come. However, this is usually rectified by the puppies themselves as they grow on, for they are able to take more from her and by so doing create a better balance. In the case of a bitch who has lost her puppies and is carrying milk to her bodily discomfort, then veterinary advice is best sought as there are suitable drugs to offset this state. Sometimes breeders are worried at seeing their bitches with milk after the puppies have been weaned. It is seldom that this condition need cause concern as the surplus will usually disperse naturally as the glands tighten up. Some breeders hasten this process by dabbing around the teat area with methylated spirits soaked into a wad of cotton wool and this seems an effective system.

AGLACTIA

The lack of milk is a somewhat different story and a worrying one for the breeder of a very promising looking litter, also for the dam herself. It is not uncommon for the whelping mother to get a high temperature and this stays the flow of her milk often for as much as thirty-six hours. Puppies need their mother's milk almost at once if they are to thrive well, and if the milkless state persists longer than six hours then some action has to be taken, apart from the constant placing of the puppies on the teats to encourage milk flow. It is important that the whelps get the colostrum which is present in their dam's milk in the early stages of its flow. This is Nature's immuniser and gives the puppies protection from disease in the first few weeks of their lives. If they fail to get this colostrum then it is better to get your veterinary surgeon to act. He will make the desired injections and give them the necessary protection. The dam herself may be injected to reduce her temperature and this usually coincides with an even and normal flow of milk.

HAND-REARING

This is a task for the dedicated breeder only. Sometimes, as already mentioned, a bitch following delivery of her puppies will have no milk; she may be too ill to care what becomes of the youngsters or refuse to attend them for a variety of reasons, probably best known to herself. At worst, she may have died in the course of whelping them or due to a Caesarian section. The breeder is then left with an orphan litter, crying out loudly for milk, which is not forthcoming. If he has foreseen such a situation, he will have arranged for a foster parent bitch to be on the way, but to come by a foster at a moment's notice is no easy task, so the alternative course of action to save the puppies is to hand-feed them. This is by no means as simple as it sounds and any person taking on this task must be prepared for at least a month of devoted attention to the puppies and quite a few sleepless nights. However, when the course of care and feeding has been completed and the litter satisfactorily reared, it will be an unusual breeder who does not survey the results of his work with justifiable pride.

'Lactol' is a good stand-by for bitch's milk. Instructions for hand-rearing will be found on the canister, but great care must be taken in the selection of the exact quantities recommended, also the actual mixing, as well as the temperature of the feeds and frequency of feeding. A fresh mixture is essential for every meal and especially for a large litter, if such is involved when constant food temperature has to be maintained. This is best achieved by keeping the cup of 'Lactol' mixture standing in a bowl of hot water. This will ensure that when the time comes to feed the last puppy, his or her food will be given at the same required heat as enjoyed by the first feeder.

Once the puppy has been fed, wipe his nose gently with a piece of damp cotton wool. This will remove any congealed milk around his nostrils and face. Normally, if the dam was on the scene she would start licking them as soon as they had fed in order to induce urination and the passing of motions. Her wet, warm and bossy tongue around their private parts would soon achieve this naturally, but as these orphans are without such maternal attentions, the result has to be achieved artifically. To simulate the bitch's method it is necessary to take a pad of cotton wool which has been dampened with *warm* water. Gently stroke over and around the puppies' parts with this and both urination and the passing of motions will be effected. Once this has proved successful, gently smear with 'Vaseline' the anus and vulva or penis of every puppy. It is important to ensure that the puppies' intestines do not become blocked so *both* motions must be passed either before or immediately following a meal. Should any puppy seem distressed, it may prove necessary to ease into the rectum for a fractional distance a well-greased clinical thermometer of the half-minute blunt end variety. This can be expected to encourage the passing of a motion.

If possible, always use an infra-red lamp when hand-rearing puppies.

This maintains a constant temperature and should be set between 24° and 26.5°C (75°–80°F) for the first three days, after which time the warmth emitted from the lamp can be reduced to 15.5°C (60°F) by raising it from floor level and easing off the warmth by going higher each day. Make certain the lamp is suspended safely from the ceiling and use a dull-emitter bulb as this type is considered safer when youngsters open their eyes, about ten days after their birth. It is as well to protect the lamp reflector with an all-round wire cage guard in case a bulb should break loose accidentally and fall on the litter.

It will be realised that puppies who have been deprived of their dam's natural milk will lack in colostrum, the protective natural fluid which contains globulin and has the effect of a mild laxative, eliminating impurities which may have accumulated in the puppies during the period of gestation. The antibodies concerned serve to immunise the youngsters against the various virus diseases which beset young canines until they are about nine or ten weeks of age. Hand-reared puppies must therefore be given an alternative form of protection in the form of gamma globulin, and here the veterinary surgeon's skill has to be employed with suitable injections.

The task of hand-rearing is one for a dedicated person. It is far from easy, and takes up considerable time, patience and occasionally a deal of frustration; but so long as regularity in feeding, correct temperature of food and surroundings, regular defecation and urination is ensured, success can be expected.

CAESARIAN SECTION

This operation is sometimes necessary if the bitch is carrying one or more large puppies or if the puppies are wrongly placed or dead within the womb. The veterinary surgeon will open the uterus and remove the puppies. The danger lies not in the actual operation, which is fairly simple from a veterinary viewpoint, but it is in the fact that the bitch is of necessity, heavily anaesthetised, which means that the unborn puppies are also anaesthetised. Being so small and weak at the unborn stage, it is often extremely difficult to get them to show signs of life after a birth by Caesarian section, and many puppies are lost for just this reason. However, many surgeons now use an advanced form of anaesthetic which does not have the effect of anaesthetising the puppies, and this may well be the answer to the loss of so many puppies through Caesarian section. The secret of making a successful operation of this kind lies largely on careful timing. The operation is best undertaken (after careful determination as to its necessity) when the bitch has commenced her labour, but before she has become panicky by ineffectual straining.

If it is to save a bitch from a very long and arduous whelping, then it is to be recommended, for the dam seldom suffers any after-effects, and is usually comfortably settled with her little family, all sucking happily at her in a matter of two or three hours after the operation. Make sure that the bitch and her puppies are very quiet and warm, as there is, of course, a certain amount of shock involved. Some breeders utilise an infra-red lamp, installed for several days, but it is more usual to introduce stone hot-water bottles, well wrapped round with pieces of blanket to prevent the bitch or her puppies being burnt. These should be placed behind her back in the whelping box and a good cosy heat will be generated.

It is not unusual to find the operation will prevent the bitch's milk coming down for several hours and should this occur it may be deemed necessary to allow the whelps some interim nourishment from 'Lactol' or similar good preparation. The milk should be made to the consistency specified for new-born puppies, details as will be written on the tin. However, in spite of the fact that there is little or no milk coming from their mother's teats, the youngsters should be deployed constantly on the teats, as their suckling will stimulate the flow and hurry it along.

The fact that a bitch has had the misfortune to suffer a Caesarian operation does not mean that she is destined for this inconvenience every time she is due to whelp. Probably at the next event she will whelp quite normally with no complication at all.

5 Feeding and Management

Weaning

The way puppies are weaned will have a lasting effect on them all their lives so it is vitally important to do this job properly and well, especially if strong and healthy Staffordshire Bull Terriers are wanted. A well-reared puppy is thus put on the right path to full health and one so started seldom suffers a set-back, even in the difficult days of his adolescence. The best time to start weaning the Stafford puppy is when he is about three-and-a-half weeks old. This applies to a puppy from an average sized litter of, say, five or six members. If the litter is perhaps eight members, then the earlier you can start weaning them with safety after three weeks of age, the better. A lot depends on the milk supply coming through from the dam. If this is adequate then your start can be more gradual.

Firstly, they have to be taught to lap. There are a number of good milk preparations on the market, 'Lactol' being an excellent example. Full instructions for its use will be found on the canister and it is adaptable to any age and weight of puppy. Usually, a heaped teaspoonful will do as a starter for each puppy and it should be mixed with hot water, just off boiling point to the consistency of thick cream, then beaten or stirred well until it appears glossy and emulsified. Then it should be brought to the consistency of thin cream by adding more hot water. Four or five teaspoons of the mixture at blood heat should then be put into a clean saucer and the puppy and its food put on to a clean dry towel. Gently push his nose into the mixture. At first he will object to this indignity and splutter and blow into it; then as the taste of it penetrates his consciousness, he will show more interest in the food, especially if a little of it is taken on to the tip of the little finger and placed between his lips. Once he has got over the initial difficulty in lapping he will soon learn how to take the food. Always serve the 'Lactol' mixture to a puppy at blood heat and try to maintain the temperature of the food by standing it in a pan of hot water during the feeding operation. Once lapping and eating has been taught, the youngsters can be put on firmer foods like light milk puddings, poached egg, minced boiled tripe and finely shredded raw butcher's meat.

So that a healthy appetite is maintained and the puppies are eager to eat, it is a good plan to make sure they have been off their dam for at least two hours previously. They will then attack the food with gusto and begin to look forward to their menu. Goat's milk can later be introduced instead of cow's milk and its value cannot be over-emphasised in view of its high fat and mineral salts content. Up to the first week of solid feeding, no doubt the puppies will have been fed individually, but it will be found by careful guidance that communal feeding can be achieved. To avoid some of the more eager ones from falling head-first into the food, it is a good idea to raise the bowl perhaps a couple of inches off ground level. Make sure that when feeding a number of lusty puppies that individuals are not allowed to hog the main part of the food. When this has been noted, allow the offenders to get their reasonable share then withdraw them and leave the way clear for their slower brothers and sisters.

After ten days of weaning the puppies should be approaching complete independence from their mother; in fact, the greater their solid food intake the less they will depend on her and when they are five weeks of age, her influence upon them should be negligible. She may want to see them once a day when they will probably rush her and snatch an impromptu drink from her now-failing supply. She will soon want to see them off however, for by this time their bulk and strength and sharp claws will be irritating her. By this time too, they will be on five proper meals a day, two or three milky ones and two with raw meat. The quantities should be staggered well to avoid distension of their stomach muscles and close watch should be kept on the bitch during her occasional visits to her litter in case she regurgitates or disgorges her own food to help in the weaning process. This might seem an unsavoury system of mothercare to humans, but it is a perfectly natural function on the bitch's part and is unlikely to do any harm to the youngsters. The main thing to do is to see that the dam gets another meal to replace what she has brought up for after doing this service she is bound to be hungry.

Now is the time to commence fattening the mother up. She has put a lot of strength and body into her puppies and reduced her own bodiment by so doing; this then needs replacement. She should be given plenty of fresh, raw meat, eggs, cheese and biscuits too, but her fluid intake should be restricted to a minimum to help the natural diminishment of the milk supply until it finally disappears. It is possible too that a tonic will help her and this can be prescribed by your veterinary surgeon. She will speedily get back into full bloom and condition if you do this. A lot of owners forget to work on the bitch at this time, so occupied are they with their valuable new arrivals. To omit this duty shows lack of planning skill, especially if she is to be mated again at next heat.

Novice breeders are frequently puzzled as to the amount of meat to give a young puppy. As a *rough*, but useful, guide the amount given at each meal should not exceed the bulk of each puppy's head. Imagine the food roughly shaped or moulded into a ball about the size of the youngster's head and skull. When the food is put down watch him eat it. If he goes through the quantity comfortably, then no doubt it suits his appetite, but if he pauses, takes a breath, then starts again, it is reasonably certain that this puppy needs only the amount of food up to the point where he paused. At six weeks of age, the puppy can have food such as Farley's Rusks, biscuits etc., as well as his normal diet.

Once the puppy has been fed on food other than his dam's milk she will stop cleaning him up. This job must be taken on by the breeder who should ensure that any motions left adhering to the anal region are cleaned off with cotton wool swabs to which have been added a few drops of 'TCP' or similar preparation.

Most Staffordshire Bull Terrier puppies are big enough and fit enough to go off to new homes by the time they are eight weeks of age. You can, in deference to the dam's feelings, stagger their departures, assuming she is still showing an interest in them, so that she does not lose them all at once. However, this may not be at all necessary and the wise owner will know and understand his bitch and make up his mind what is best for her. Most, if not all, bitches are usually quite pleased to see the back of their litters by the time eight weeks have passed!

Feeding the adult dog

It is important to remember that the best quality feeding is in the long run an investment and an economy. The money spent on good food and attention to feeding generally is likely to offset to quite a considerable degree the outlay for medicines and veterinary bills. A sound diet must contain a correct proportion of protein, carbohydrates and fats. Meat, eggs, fish and cheese etc. supply the proteins; cereal, biscuits, bread etc. the carbohydrates, while fats are assimilated from the usual sources of milk, butter content, fish oils and the fat on meat, etc. The aim in feeding is to develop and preserve a dog in good health, in good bloom and with an equable and contented frame of mind. The dog's food must therefore be balanced, varied and of the highest standard. With all dogs, mealtimes are the important events of the day. Consequently, to give a dog a meal which will benefit him to the full, some careful thought must be applied to the matter.

There is not much extra work involved in careful preparation of a dog's meal. Cut up the meat into pieces of manageable size. A dog does not masticate his food in the same way as a human. Most of the breaking-up and dissolving of his food is effected by strong gastric juices in the stomach. Too large lumps of meat might cause choking; pieces which are too small, such as minced meat – perhaps suitable for very young puppies – do not allow the mature animal's gastric juice ample play. Raw, fresh meat is better than cooked, for none of the natural nutriments have been simmered away. Observe scrupulous hygiene with the feeding vessels used; dirty plates and dishes harbour disease, and in any case it is only fair and just to the dog to make his meals palatable and well-presented.

With most adult dogs, one main meal in the evening, possibly with a few dry biscuits at midday, constitutes the best form of feeding. Many dogs prefer raw meat and thrive on flesh in this form, but there are good alternatives available in canned form. These are prepared hygienically, and producers are well aware of the valuable market available and ready to meet it with food which is well fortified with vitamins and minerals to meet the special requirements of dogs. A wide range of such canned dog food is to be seen on retailers' shelves and it is a good idea to let your dog run through the best-known of these to ascertain the kind he fancies best. Then you can keep to this, with only an occasional change. By doing this, the dog will look forward to his dinners and develop a good appetite in advance of them. The same system should apply to biscuits which supply carbohydrates, there being many makes and kinds on the market, not all of them perhaps palatable to individual dogs. A saucer of milk with the biscuits at tea-time will be appreciated, but fresh, cool water should be available to the dog at *all* times during the day. It is

Flash Scobie of Cradbury, owned by Fred Phillips.

Beaconmoor Dicky Minty,
owned by Mrs A. Mitchell.

normally found provident not to give food to a dog just before retiring, but a small knob of cheese to please him and supply added vitamins will be beneficial. Bones, but only large raw marrow or knuckle bones, are useful for keeping the teeth clean and healthy also to stimulate gastric juices and to offer a good supply of vitamins and calcium from the marrow.

The type of meat to use is the best you can afford. Meat 'unfit for human consumption' is not fit for pedigree dog consumption either. Knacker's meat comes from an animal which has died, probably from some unknown cause. It may be almost rotten before it reaches your dog's feeding bowl and it may well be full of veterinary drugs unlikely to do him anything but harm. The heart of ox or sheep is good and ox cheek and ox liver have their uses and values. Tripe and the various forms of offal are considerably less in worth; paunch, although recommended by some breeders (possibly because of its cheapness), has little value compared with fresh, raw meat. Steamed white fish, carefully boned, is excellent and herrings, when in season, cooked in a pressure cooker, give considerable nourishment.

The average grown Staffordshire Bull Terrier needs *at least* 500g (1lb) of raw, fresh meat daily. If you cannot manage this, then certainly no less than 250g (½lb) and you should then make up the volume with some other form of food. If you want a good-looking, healthy dog with bright eyes and glossy coat and loads of vigour, do not attempt any economies in feeding, for good food and attention are an insurance.

From the age of six or seven months, the forward puppy can be fed as an adult. The main meal should be in the evening and concentration should always be on the feeding at this time, given preferably after his exercise or field work. Managed this way, he will gain the full nutritive effects of his food while sleeping and his digestion will be orderly. Always feed an adult Staffordshire *dry*, for soft mushy food is of no use if you want to achieve best results. Never feed or water after heavy exercise, such as a ratting expedition, a training session or a fight. Let the dog settle: first return him to normal respiration, then give him a drink, followed by food if a meal time is approaching.

It is probably a good idea to get your dog used to a variety of foods, i.e. raw meat, cooked meat (not too much of this), boiled also steamed fish, proprietary canned meats, processed forms and so on. Horsemeat should be avoided and so should meat unfit for human consumption, as stated above, unless of course there is an emergency which demands special feeding. By giving your dog such a variety you insure against him becoming too fastidious and turning up his nose at anything but raw meat. When a dog rejects any food but his favourite meat, it becomes a worry to feed him for it is not always practicable or convenient to produce just what he wants for every meal. This is why a dog should be trained in feeding, just as he is trained in other things.

Be careful with rabbit; the flesh is highly nutritive, but it should be eaten immediately after the animal has been caught, for the bones are springy and dangerous following the first day. Never allow the dog to have poultry or game to eat; the bones are needle-like and many a dog has choked on these, or had his gullet pierced. During winter months, always pour a teaspoonful of coarse cod-liver oil on the dog's food, or maybe he will be pleased to lick the measure off a large spoon to avoid spilling. The main aim in dog-rearing is to produce a 'good-doer' which is a dog who does well however casually treated; one who eats well, requires no special treatment and has always thrived from birth. If you have one such as this, you are fortunate indeed.

Puppy diet sheets

Always make sure that the new owners of your puppies have suitable diet sheets. Even owners who have had previous experience of puppy rearing should have one, for it is easy enough to forget the art and routine. Lists of recommended foods and feeding times are always appreciated and it is important to know how and on what a new puppy has been fed, so that the sudden change of ownership is not made too dramatic. A simple feeding programme for a Stafford puppy is given below:

8.30 am   Bread and milk, cereal and milk, light porridge, etc. Make sure milk is warm, never hot.
12.30 pm   Chopped meat meal. Mix with warm gravy made from Oxo, Bovril or similar – broth is ideal. Wholemeal or brown breed rusks soaked in gravy or in boiled vegetable liquor can be added. Rusks are made from bread by baking slices in the oven.
4.30 pm   Warm milk meal or rusks and gravy.
8.30 pm   Repeat the 12.30 pm meat meal.

The meat should be chopped to a useful size, but not minced. Some breeders shred it, but better results are achieved when the dog's gastric juices are brought into full play. Minced meat will not bring the digestive system into full action; although even more care is needed to ensure that the meat is not chopped too chunkily, for this could cause a gobbling youngster to choke.

While the puppy is young it will help bone formation to sprinkle a little powdered calcium on his food. Your veterinary surgeon or pharmacist will advise on the quantity and best form to use; this being applied over the evening meal. Do not give ordinary vegetables to a puppy under six months of age, although vegetable juice extract obtained by cooking carrots, endives and turnip tops, poured over a meal is first class for Vitamin A application as well as being rich in iodine and mineral salts.

VITAMINS

A number of conditions and diseases are caused through vitamin deficiency. Vitamins are essential to a dog's good health and essential vitamins are present in natural feeding or through the medium of grass, grazing and sunshine etc. In the right amounts they give the dog's body all the basic nutrients he needs for goodness and contentment. Modern feeding, however, is often suspect and at times one is inclined to doubt its efficacy in this respect.

Vitamin A: Present in fish-liver oils, heart and liver, eggs and milk. It is useful in building up resistance to infection and can build strong bone in young stock. It is stated to be useful in avoiding eye infections and a factor against night-blindness. Raw carrots and parsley are rich in Vitamin A.

Vitamin B: Often referred to as B complex, thereby embracing a number of factors. It is present in milk, meat and eggs, also in liver, yeast and wheat-germ. It strengthens the nervous system and maintains a healthy skin and coat. There are proprietary Vitamin B tonics on the market which can be injected, but the use of these must be confirmed by a competent veterinary surgeon.

Vitamin C: Stated to be the 'sunshine' vitamin and obtainable from grass and some berries. It will aid the body to resist infection and it is essential for growth, good teeth and gums and healthy skin. Milk too, contains this vitamin. Note that this is a water-soluble vitamin and is not stored by the body which means that a course entails daily dosage.

Vitamin D: This is found in fish-oils (especially halibut-liver oil), egg yolk, butter and liver. It is another 'sunshine' vitamin and is essential for supporting the two minerals needed for good health – calcium and phosphorus. This useful vitamin is an enemy of rickets and similar bone deficiency conditions.

Vitamin E: Wheat-germ oil is the main source of this vitamin which has an important bearing on fertility in the dog and bitch. An active stud dog can manage well at his job if he has been reared from puppyhood on Vitamin E, for it will maintain his potency and delay advance of possible sterility. When given to the bitch, the chances of dead puppies or absorbed foetuses during pregnancy will be brought to a minimum. Vitamin E Succinate and Wheat-Germ Oil capsules are useful means of dosing.

The clever breeder will incorporate a proper balance of vitamins and minerals in his application to preserve good all-round health in his Staffordshire Bull Terrier. So long as the dog is allowed fresh meat, fish, milk and eggs with easy access to sunshine and clean, green grass grazing, he is unlikely to go wrong in health. Some meat fat will benefit him as this is strong in Vitamins A and D. There are good proprietary conditioners on the market in the form of yeast tablets. These contain vitamins and minerals blended for puppy, dog and bitch alike.

Training

The true Staffordshire Bull Terrier is a high-powered member of the popular Bull breeds family; he is strong, athletic, virile and fully endowed with superior canine intelligence and determination. Such a fine temperament needs moulding while in the course of his development and this is why most people prefer a small puppy to an adult, for the former can be trained much more simply and to its owner's specific requirements. Firm training is essential; unfortunately, a lot of owners fail to apply rules and regulations to their dogs until too late. Many seem to think that a small puppy rushing pell-mell about the house, knocking down this, ruining that, is a comic circus turn for the family circle. It might be for a short time, but only while the puppy is small – it becomes far from funny when the dog is mature and remains untrained.

A poorly trained dog reflects upon his owner's aptitude as a trainer. The first word a young dog must learn is 'No!' It is an easy word to say and easy for a dog to understand its implication, also it is true that most puppies are willing and eager to learn it. Never thrash a puppy; this is a fatal move in training and not many beaten dogs ever regain confidence in the person who beat them, quite apart from the fact that a beaten dog will seldom respond properly thereafter. Corporal punishment, when it has to be applied, is better administered with a rolled-up newspaper. Keep it handy always but use it sparingly. It will make a lot of noise, but never hurt. The young dog will hate it, but he is unlikely to bear any malice about it. The clap it makes when making contact should be synchronised with the word 'No!' In a very short time it will be completely unnecessary to use it – the word itself will suffice or even the mere showing of the newspapers will do. By this simple and humane method a youngster can be gently persuaded to stop biting furniture and nibbling ankles, and to lie down and stop making a nuisance of himself. Just show him what to do in the simplest, most commonsense method adaptable to the problem and he will learn quite quickly.

HOUSE TRAINING

Training a small puppy to be clean in the home has always been a problem for the new owner; even a deterrent to ownership by some house-proud people. It need never be, for it is simple to house-break a puppy in a very short time. Puppies of just two months of age sleep a great deal, just like babies. They should be allowed to do this as often as they wish and children should be taught never to disturb them while they rest. Quite apart from a small dog requiring ample sleep to store up energy, even the mildest natured dog must be hard put to retain good humour when pummelled suddenly out of a deep sleep.

When a puppy has had enough sleep he will open his eyes; as soon as the eyes are open he will want to urinate. That is certain, and it is the pattern to watch, for then he should be taken up or guided either to the garden or to his sand tray. If it is to be out of doors, then close the door on him and watch him until he has squatted and completed the job. Then open the door and let him in – not before, however much he might complain about being shut out. If he has to use a sand or dirt tray, then keep him within the perimeter of the tray until he has finished, then ceremoniously (almost), lift him off. A few lessons such as this will find the idea well embedded in his mind and before long, the instant he opens his eyes from a sleep he will move to the terrain beyond the garden door or the sand tray to do his business. Be sure to praise him when he is good and only the mildest scold when he is not, for he is bound to make one or two mistakes while learning. Never scold him if he makes one or two puddles indoors because the door was not opened fast enough to let him get outside when nature was calling urgently. To punish him for something which is really the owner's fault is patently unfair and may well cause a set-back in his training.

It is probable that he will forget himself at night in any case. Small puppies are continually making puddles – their bladders are quite weak at two or even three months of age. The best plan is to cover the floor of his pen, or the kitchen where he sleeps with newspapers, then in the morning these can be gathered up and put into the disposal bin with the minimum of fuss. While the youngster is learning to be clean, of course, to leave him in rooms with valuable carpets or curtains would be foolish in the extreme. Any untrained animal should be kept where he can do no damage to property and fitments. If a puppy tears up one's best carpet slippers or rips open a cushion or two, never blame the pup; it is the fault of the person who left him there unattended with such temptation!

ON THE LEAD

The next step is to get the young dog used to collar and lead. Naturally, he should not be taken on to the sidewalk and the streets until he has had all his inoculations. Too many health hazards exist where older dogs have paraded. Lamp-posts especially seem to harbour diseases, yet they hold a traditional fascination for dogs of all ages. For this reason, it is best to give the puppy his *elementary* lead training in the home and garden.

A cheap collar should be purchased initially for he will soon grow out of his first collar and it will have to be discarded. Buy a light-weight, narrow, strap-like collar with lead to match. The youngster should be trained to accept this collar by putting it on for short, then progressively longer periods, until he finally accepts it. At first, he will probably scratch at it with some irritation and annoyance, but eventually it will be tolerated all day with little or no fuss. By wearing a collar he will become more manageable, but it should be removed at night while he sleeps as if left on it will disarrange the smoothness of the coat around the neck and cause an unsightly ruff of hair.

Later, when the puppy finds the collar comfortable and to his taste, a light lead can be attached to it and he can be encouraged to walk up and down. He will not like the idea very much and will probably emulate a captured trout on the end of a line, but with some reassurance coupled with the owner's patience, he will learn to move composedly back and forth. Do not forget to use a titbit or two in the course of the training, giving him one every time he behaves well. Watch for the puppy which pulls excessively and tries to dash too far ahead of his trainer or handler. This will detract from the correct development of his shoulders, quite apart from the annoyance it will give his trainer. Keep early training to periods of about ten minutes duration to save the puppy getting bored. If he pulls too much, tap him across the extended muzzle with a rolled-up newspaper. Jerk back the lead at the same time as you tap him with the command 'Heel' or 'Back'. He will soon learn not to pull. A puppy which on the other hand drags back, squats in a stubborn fashion and digs his feet into the ground, so to speak, has to be encouraged forward with tasty morsels, plus a determined pull forward on the lead which should bring him into action. With puppies destined for the show ring, it is wise to train them to move on either side of the handler, but when obedience work is the aim, then always keep the pupil on the handler's *left* side.

Exercise

A healthy Staffordshire Bull Terrier needs a lot of exercise. He is quite capable of doing six times and more the amount that his equally healthy owner would normally seek and still be ready for more. Make sure he is never let off his lead where traffic is a hazard. Even the best trained ones sometimes fall foul of fast cars. The open fields and parks are best for free running off the lead. In such confines a ball game can be held without much fear that the dog will come into trouble. Watch should be kept for other dogs, of course, making sure that no mischief is made

NZ Ch. Wellwisher of Wystaff, owned by Mrs Marion Forester.

either by him or against him. Lakesides are probably kept clear of, for some Staffords like a swim, although I must admit I have never owned one which does. Ponds etc. do make for wet dogs in the car, and sometimes hold water which is stagnant and probably bad for a canine's health.

A dog being conditioned for show work needs to be hard. Walk him several miles a day over rough ground, even cinder tracks, for this will harden the feet, pads and strengthen the pasterns, quite apart from giving benefit to the hindquarters. Keep an eye open for hills and slopes. Throw the ball up their inclines and let the dog retrieve it. The 'push' he has to give his hindquarters to get to the top will help greatly to develop his hind muscles and at the same time trim down to a minimum his toe-nails. Although free running exercise is good for him, exercise on the lead is better. It maintains steadiness and rhythm of gait, which develops elegant deportment which will hold the dog in good stead when he enters the show ring. He should be trained always to 'walk' on the lead – this means that the lead from owner's hand to dog's collar should be slack, never taut. Once the dog gets used to being on the lead and accepting its instructive pressures he will enjoy his perambulations and achieve a natural action which must be encouraged.

Never over-walk a young puppy for this can do irreparable harm. Exercise is the second important need to a Stafford – the first being food, of course. Therefore, when it is pouring outside with rain, do not be

Yankeestaff Bolivar, owned by Mrs Nancy Malec.

tempted to deprive him of his daily walk, however put-off you may be at the thought of getting wet. Take him out and when you return ensure he is dried down well and towelled properly underneath – then he will come to no harm. No one should buy a dog unless he intends to maintain that dog's fitness by feeding the animal properly and giving it ample and regular exercise.

A fat Staffordshire Bull Terrier is neither a delight to look at nor does he enjoy life. A dog gets best results from his exercise when he is walked alone, but it is obvious that someone owning a number of dogs cannot do this and will need help when exercising. Always be aware that one dog will get another into trouble; it being true that with two dogs, one has the nucleus of a pack! If a dog or dogs are walked in public, the handler must know that he is in control should an emergency arise. One sometimes sees a youngster out exercising a fine Stafford dog. This is wrong – an adult should be at the other end of the lead, so that the dog is under control as all dogs should be when on the public highway. Indoors, it is a different matter for temptation likely to precipitate a serious incident is unlikely to arise.

Swimming

Water-shy Staffords are a rarity, although it is not often that you see one really enjoying a prolonged swim. Even so, the keenest swimmers seem to avoid with dainty and fastidious steps, any puddle which confronts them! It is reasonably easy to get a Stafford into water, although with some it is necessary to cast a stick or ball into the water and exhort them to retrieve it. Should a dog prove obstinate, the best method is to employ a trained and keen water dog (of any breed) as an example to the pupil.

Guarding the home

Some Staffordshire Bull Terriers are speedier than others in learning this valuable lesson. Most of the Bull breeds are perhaps a little slow at learning guard work – many of them being too much of the 'hail-fellow-well-met' mentality when it comes to meeting strangers. This attitude can persist right into their second year up to the age of eighteen months. It should occasion no concern, for once a dog has learnt to guard the home, the ability shown proves that the waiting period was worthwhile.

A young puppy can have some elementary training in the work providing the owner is prepared to put in a little 'acting' to achieve results. Get someone outside to ring the bell or knock on the door or window. The average puppy will at once cock an ear and listen – he is at once surprised and aware. At this point, the owner should make the best imitation he can of a dog's bark – 'Woof', he will say and no matter how foolish he may feel in delivering this sound, he should come in again with another 'Woof', the more menacing and intense tone it sounds, the better. The puppy will probably catch on to this after a few tries and before long as soon as the bell rings or the knocker is assaulted he will 'Woof' too! Once he has started to bark, he will get enthusiastic, especially if encouraged and the lesson will soon sink in; certainly such lessons are seldom forgotten.

Remember too that when the dog is older and likely to appear fearsome to a stranger, he should be taken to the door every time one calls. It is suggested that a strap collar should be kept on him all day. As the owner opens the door with one hand he should 'hold back' the dog with the other. The dog himself will almost certainly be thrusting towards the opened door and the visitor and the whole effect to the stranger will be one of a fearsome-looking dog trying to get at him. Most would-be intruders when they know a householder has a resident Staffordshire Bull Terrier will divert their attentions elsewhere.

Pub owners are advised to let their late-night customers see the dog, but not make friends with it. The dog should not run free outside the bar, but show himself just before closing time on the serving side. The more fearsome he looks and acts the better.

Bathing

An adult Stafford needs very few baths, a small puppy none. This rule is dependent, of course, on the animal not having encountered any obnoxious substance which has made his proximity unpleasant or having got covered with mud. In such cases, whatever the age of the dog, a bath is essential. The dog's coat contains natural oils and too much bathing will remove some of these, it taking quite a few days to return to normal. Regular attention with a brush and comb and houndglove every day is much better (see opposite). However, when applying the brush, go through the dog's coat and body carefully from muzzle to tail. Check his eyes, his skin and ears – make sure the body harbours no parasites, especially where the tail sets on.

When bathing a Stafford, ensure that the water is just warm. An over-hot bath will upset the dog and make him quite unco-operative next time you want to put him in the tub. He should not have been fed within two or three hours of being bathed and certainly given a chance to relieve himself first. The wise owner will have made sure that everything he wants for the dog's bath is close at hand. The items needed are two rough Turkish terry towels, one to soak off the initial moisture, the other to remove the dampness and to ensure complete dryness underneath the dog and around his most tender parts. If you can arrange the positioning of the bath where he has a chance to shake himself, so much the better for then you will soak the towels much less.

A good dog shampoo can be used and today a number of reliable makes exist on the market. Use the one you choose according to instructions, but make sure that every vestige is removed when rinsing time is over or the coat may cloy in parts and cause the dog some irritation. Extra care should be given when bringing the shampoo near to the dog's eyes and his ears. Some owners smear a little petroleum jelly around the eyes and insert a jelly-smeared cotton wool wad in the dog's ears for safety. It seems almost unnecessary to warn owners that all such grease and wads *must* be disposed of when the bath is over. It is vital that the dog is dried off completely. The parts to heed particularly are soft-flesh areas in the underparts, the genitals and between the toes. Rub down well around the loins too. Let the dog remain in an even temperature for a while – on no account let him go out of doors too soon.

Int. Ch. Bracken of Judael, owned by Mr B. Preston.

Grooming

The healthy Staffordshire in good bloom needs very little grooming, especially if he gets a daily application of the brush or houndglove to his coat. However, most exhibitors like to 'dolly up' their dogs before a show and a little extra gloss to a dog's coat can do nothing but good. The brush or glove will stimulate his muscles too and make him feel perky – that is why some exhibitors are seen busy with grooming tools even at the ringside! It all goes to bring the dog into the ring 'on his toes'. The best type of brush for the Stafford coat is one of semi-hard bristle. Any good pet supplies shop will advise. A good quality houndglove is well recommended and this can be used comfortably even at odd moments. A large chamois leather is also an advantage for this will finish off with a high gloss effect. Check on the dog's lips if it is a hot day to remove any

The Malasa Mauler, owned by Messrs Shelley and Thompson.

saliva; then ensure the dog's eyes and rims are clean and free from undue moisture. The ears should be inspected and cleaned around with cotton wool. Inspect under the tail and make sure that the anal region is clean and free from residue. Some exhibitors trim the 'feather' below the tail, and this needs to be done carefully as many dogs are left with a ragged tail. Executed in a correct fashion, the desired 'rat-tail' mode can be achieved and the show dog made to look very smart and slick.

Fighting

The Staffordshire Bull Terrier was evolved as a fighting dog, as is generally known. When he was matched dog against dog in the pit, it was not infrequent that they would fight to the death. Clearly, then, aggressiveness is an important ingredient in this breed's make-up. The possession of it gives the dog the will to attack his selected opponent and to press home any advantage he may achieve. If the fighting dog lacked the attribute of aggressiveness, then it is unlikely he would last very long. However, the breed as such is unique, for the *true* Stafford, while possessing the attribute seldom evinces this 'quality' unless he is called upon to do so. The character of the breed is not to fight unprovoked, but when provoked to fight to the death. Thus, although a good dog is endowed inherently with aggressiveness, he will not make a nuisance of himself (as is usual with some other breeds in which aggressiveness is a fault) unless he finds it necessary to protect himself or his owner.

The good Stafford knows how to take care of trouble if it is forced upon him, just as he knows how to select friend from foe. Staffordshires love the family circle and most will willingly die in defence of those they have learned to love. However, sometimes even the best humoured dog is sorely tried in his patience. He might be out with his master, enjoying a peaceful walk in the park when he is attacked by some unruly canine. It is little wonder that he retaliates and then comes the job of separating them.

With strong dogs this is sometimes far from easy, but when one remembers that in most cases it is usual (although not invariable) for only one of the combatants to have a hold, the task becomes easier for a single person, although to have a helping friend around is much better. The loose dog, i.e. the one which has no hold, should be raised from the ground so that he cannot push in with his hindquarters. The biting dog's loins should then be trapped between the knees of the second person, who should slide his right hand (knuckles facing down) underneath the collar, grab and twist the leather, all the time bringing pressure to bear on the biter's windpipe with the other hand. This position may require to be held for a few moments up to the point when the dog with the hold will need to inhale, whereupon there will be a split second of relaxation in the bite. At this point, he can be dragged off, although it is wise to watch now that the loose dog does not seize the hands of his helper or rush back into the fray and grab his adversary, when it will all start again!

As has been stressed previously, it is important to keep thin, strap-like collars on all the Staffordshire Bull Terriers around you throughout the day. Without such a collar on a fighting Stafford it would be virtually impossible to choke him off, for the dog in action fills out his body and neck steel hard with muscle when in battle. This is a hereditament from the days when as a fighting dog he used this natural 'armour plate' method for protection.

Elementary training in obedience work

It is never too early to commence training a Stafford. At eight weeks of age, a good deal of sense exists in that unique headpiece. The average puppy is anxious to learn that he can relate well with his owner. The master will get pleasure in owning a dog which will do what he is told, and the dog will enjoy himself better because he knows that he has pleased his master. This is as it should be – a happy rapport between dog and master. Training a small puppy must inevitably be of the gradual kind. A puppy over-worked in the scheme of training becomes stale and bored with it all; such a youngster seldom becomes a successful pupil. Not more than ten minutes at a time should be devoted to training a puppy. At all times he should be treated kindly, intelligently and with commonsense. The occasional titbit reward for good results is essential and this should be accompanied with a pat on the head and a few words of praise.

The following exercises are recommended for the welfare of the pet Staffordshire Bull Terrier, making him a welcome member of the family circle, knowing how to behave and becoming unobtrusive when required by his master. If he shows exceptional prowess at obedience work then he might even be considered for advanced courses which would allow him to enter obedience tests which are held by some canine societies in conjunction with their own dog-show events. There are also registered training clubs which hold Obedience Dog Shows under Kennel Club rules, and although such bodies aim at standards demanding high canine intelligence, there is no reason at all why the average Staffordshire Bull Terrier cannot achieve top honours in this fascinating pursuit and hobby.

'COME' WHEN CALLED

This is a lesson which a dog *must* learn. Any Staffordshire Bull Terrier who does not know when to come when called is an embarrassment, even a liability to his owner as well as being an unhappy dog in the bargain. It is always best to start a training session with the pupil hungry. He will then be more appreciative of the titbit rewards which can be won for achievement.

The lesson can be arranged with either one tutor, or two. It is probably quicker taught and more effective with two. Let one person hold the youngster and the other at, say, ten yards distance, call it by name, gently adding 'Come!' The puppy will probably move at once to the caller, who should praise him, pat him and award a tasty titbit. This move should then be followed by the same procedure from the helper calling 'Come!' When the puppy has gone away at the second call, he will get another word of praise, another titbit for his good work.

This formula repeated a dozen or more times from one person to the other and back again will soon sink into the youngster's consciousness. It should then be tried by one of the instructors when the puppy is half-way back to the other. He should call 'Come!' and if the puppy turns around in his tracks and returns, then the praise should be lavish and the titbit an extra good one. Should he not track back but continue to the other person, then he must not be rewarded or praised. Perhaps this will confuse him initially, but he will soon learn after a few more examples. It is best to give at least a dozen lessons to each movement, and to repeat for three consecutive days allowing ample time for the lesson to be learnt.

It is normal to give initial instruction in the precincts of the home or kennel. Not so many distractions exist here as out of doors, so the puppy will learn quicker. However, it is more important for the training to have good effect away from the youngster's usual haunts and as soon as he seems ready for the final phase of this lesson he should be taken to a local park or field. Tie a training cord, which can be twenty feet long, to his collar and hold the other end. Release him and puppy-like he will make a bee-line for some interesting object – a tree, a pond or another dog. As he nears the end of the now running-out cord which you hold, call 'Come!' It is likely in his excitement that he will be quite heedless of the command and run on, only to be turned head over heels when the cord reaches its extremity. This sudden upset will prove an unpleasant surprise, but it will make him think. After it has been repeated a few times he will halt in his rush as soon as he hears you call 'Come!' Soon, remembering his starting lesson with this command, he will turn around and walk back to you. This will be the lesson learnt and following a few more tests to ensure that it has 'sunk in', the next simple lesson can be started.

'SIT'
With official obedience training in mind, a dog should be taught always to sit on the handler's left side, hard by the handler's heels when he halts. The dog should be walked on a slack lead, his body close by the holder's left leg. A titbit held in the hand will keep his attention rapt and he will not pull away or be distracted. With the command 'Sit!' the handler should halt suddenly in his tracks, at the same instant swinging his body round to the left without moving his feet. As you do this, the dog should automatically sit. If he carries on walking, snap the lead back firmly from your stationary position, making the dog sit back on his haunches. When he does this, either naturally, or forced by the snap-back method, he should be praised and patted. This will encourage him to do it again. If difficulty is experienced in achieving a sitting position, the dog can be persuaded by taking the collar in the right hand, pulling back a little and at the same time (with the left hand) pat him down into a sit. If it is found that when he learns to sit on command he sits rather wide of your left leg you might feel inclined to move towards him; this is wrong – you should move away from him even more. Then you should encourage him to narrow the gap with your left hand and some cajolery.

'DOWN'
This exercise can be usefully employed as part two of the 'Sit' lesson.

Thus, when you have a dog fully taught to obey that command, it is already half-way to the completion of the 'Down' lesson. The best method is again with the pupil on the trainer's left side and the lead under his left foot, its end held high in his right hand. As the command 'Down!' is given in a firm tone, the lead is pulled with the right hand; this will cause the dog to be pressed down from the neck end, while with your left hand you can press down on his rear section.

'STAY'

This is an important exercise and for simplicity in training, it is best to let the exercise follow the mastery of the 'Down' position, as this is the most relaxed attitude the pupil can hold if he is to be in one spot for an extended period. Having given the command 'Down!' and on being obeyed, the trainer should now stand in front of him – you can point to the spot where he has downed, if you wish to emphasize the command 'Stay!', as you move back one step. If the dog is restless and gets up to follow you, get him immediately into the 'Down' position. Try again, and eventually he will understand that he has to remain there even with a number of yards between you. It is best to make the initial practice still holding his lead. This will allow you a few test steps back; a check can be used to play for safety over a long distance. Soon, you will be able to disappear from the dog's view while he remains in the 'Stay' position.

'HEEL'

This is really no more than basic lead training, which has already been covered in the appropriate section. However, it should be remembered that the command 'Heel!' is a useful one and one which appears readily understood by the dog. With the dog on the trainer's left side, the lead held in his right hand, a slack loop should be maintained under the dog's neck; in effect, there should be no tautness or tension in the lead. Dog and trainer should start off together with the command 'Heel!' The speed of the movement should be gauged so that the lead remains slack and the dog is hard by the trainer's heel at all times. Give the pupil plenty of praise for good results and an occasional titbit. Later, when he is adept, he can be tried without the restrictive confinement of the lead. This is the 'heel free' exercise. If he does not appear ready for this at first attempt he should be put back on the lead and given further basic training.

Points to remember include that it is important that the pupil has complete confidence in his tutor; for this reason, make sure that the dog is not scolded unnecessarily. A violent show of impatience on your part can set back many hours of progress. If you make a mistake with any instruction put it right immediately and, if the dog seems confused, make a fuss of him. If the dog fails to perform satisfactorily in an exercise which he has done previously with perfection, do not let him get away with it. Get him back to the task at once and you will probably find he does it perfectly. Dogs are quick to take advantage and any slackness condoned while training can delay progress. Watch always for individual reactions in pupils. A method used to train one might well prove totally unsuited to another. If this should be noted never use it if the pupil finds it unpleasant or fails to learn from its application.

Car travel

Always get a dog used to car travel or public transport right from puppyhood. Once he has had all his inoculations he can be taken out in a car either before his meal or at least two hours after it, the reason for this being that he is not so easily induced to actual sickness. With a full stomach before a journey a dog will suffer nausea and either slobber or vomit within a short time of starting off. It is usually those dogs who have been sick in a car who *think* they are going to be sick every time they enter a vehicle thereafter. Providing the puppy can have a few consecutive trips without being sick he is unlikely to experience nausea in future outings.

It is important, therefore, to try and avoid sickness on his first car journey. The best way to do this is to have a companion with you who will take the puppy on his lap. The initial run out should be one of short duration. If the puppy looks uncomfortable and begins to open and close his jaws spasmodically, it is a sign that he feels sick. Stop the car until he has settled down or walk or carry him back home. It will be found that the car trips can be increased in mileage each time out until quite a lengthy trip can be made without the dog feeling ill. By this time there is a good chance that he will have been cured of the weakness.

For chronic cases of car sickness there are effective drug remedies on the market which your veterinary surgeon should be asked to prescribe for a Staffordshire Bull Terrier, according to the age of your subject.

Needless noise

The Stafford, in common with others in the Bull breeds family, is not an unnecessary barker. However, one occasionally encounters a puppy which barks or howls so incessantly as to constitute a nuisance to owner and neighbours alike. Small puppies cannot understand why they should not make such a noise, so the best method of correction has to be largely psychological. The youngster must be made to learn that every time he opens his mouth to bark or scream for no reason at all, that something unpleasant happens! When he realises this he will think twice before he starts up again for fear that it will trigger off the 'treatment'.

An effective training method is to wait quietly outside the door of the room where he is kept. As soon as he barks without reason, burst open the door and shout 'No!' or 'Quiet!' Taken by surprise, he will gape at you and stop barking. Retire at once and again wait outside, waiting for the next howl to start up. Almost before it leaves his mouth be in there with the shout of 'No!' or 'Quiet!' The youngster will not like this at all, even less if the admonition is accompanied by a firm tap from a rolled-up newspaper! After a few sessions of this performance, the puppy will usually give it up as a bad job and retire the loser to his box to muse upon the strange ways of humans!

Unless the pupil is quite stupid, of course, he will learn quickly not to be so vociferous and it is important that he does, for this bad habit in a dog is a great patience tester. A danger exists, of course, that a puppy which has been trained out of needless barking will not bark a valid warning when required to do so, such as when a fire breaks out or an intruder is heard and threatens. However, most Staffordshires are sensible enough to know when their vocal services are required to guard themselves and home, so no worry should be experienced on this point. In any case, training bad habits out of a puppy normally does the growing-up individual a favour and does not destroy his natural attributes.

Jumping-up

Few canine habits annoy so much as the one which makes a dog bound straight out of a muddy garden puddle straight into the lap of a guest, ruining their new clothes and bespattering all around with filth! Such a dog reflects at once upon his owner's aptitude as a trainer and clearly such an irritating habit as this must be broken. Obviously, the first thing is to ensure at all times that muddy dogs never encounter guests, but even the best laid plans go astray and it is as well to prepare some corrective remedy for the next incident.

Patently, the jumper must be pushed quite forcefully away from his target as he leaps. Shout 'Down!' or 'No!' at him – very loudly if it is to prove effective, for the boisterous dog hears very little when excited and he needs to be halted in his tracks. If the persistent jumper takes little heed of the command, press down on his back paws as you give the command. If this proves fruitless, then bring up one knee and let him bound and bounce against that. It will almost certainly topple him over backwards and he will find it most unpleasant. A few lessons of this sort are calculated to quieten him down and mend his jumping ways.

Tail-chasing

This is an unfortunate habit which should be stopped as soon as it is noted. There are various reasons put forward for it. One is psychological, relating to boredom. The dog who is left alone for long periods with nothing to do, commences tail-chasing as a sport or diversion. Another reason (and probably the more reasonable one) is that the tip of the tail or the 'thumb-mark' to be seen a short way up from the tip, becomes irritated, either by the arrival of some parasite or skin-itch. The dog, in his discomfort chases the tail, sometimes seizing it momentarily and thereby breaking the skin or even nipping off the tail extremity if the symptom is extreme. When this occurs the irritation becomes even more acute and the tail-chasing chronic. If not halted at once it becomes truly psychological and, what might have appeared initially a sort of funny circus turn, develops into a serious condition which has been known to result in a dog being condemned.

The dog's tail must be examined throughout its whole length, right up to the set-on, to establish whether fleas or similar parasites have taken residence there. If they have, then it is obvious that their removal must be speedy. Tail-chasing can be caused by irritation anywhere in the dog's nether regions and it is important to watch the dog in his circling to detect the part of his body which seems to concern him. Sometimes the anal glands need attention; occasionally incomplete elimination of the faeces or even constipation cause soreness and distress. All such factors need to be checked as the dog cannot tell you what ails him so you have to find the answer yourself and apply the appropriate remedy. Should the tail-chasing have reached formidable proportions before any treatment has been attempted, a considerable time will need to be expended with the dog in an effort to direct his interest and attention away from the habit. It is unlikely that he will grow out of it, so he has to be encouraged or trained out of it.

Games

Once a Staffordshire Bull Terrier has left the small puppy stage, lethal toys like rubber balls and bones should be discarded. The young dog has very strong jaws and the natural tendency is for his bite to become stronger. Toys, such as those described, might last a Spaniel all its life, but are soon ripped to pieces by a strong Stafford and are dangerous, if swallowed. Bones have their dangers too. The safest are the big marrow bones, their size usually preventing a young dog getting his jaws around them, and because of their substance will not splinter. Generally speaking, avoid giving bones, although they do help a lot at teething time earlier on. There exists a danger when a young Stafford has a predisposition towards an undershot jaw for too much gnawing on a bone could well aggravate the tendency.

If you have room, suspend an old tyre by rope from a tree branch. It

The late Tom Walls, actor, at play with some of his famous 'Looe' Staffordshire Bull Terriers.

should hang just high enough from the ground to allow a Stafford to jump and grab hold and hang, swinging free. The breed as such loves this type of exercise, but individuals need to be watched as they hang on too long and do themselves harm. However, in the normal way it is a wonderful form of exercise for the breed, developing jaw, cheek and neck muscles in a most useful way. Stick games are popular and most dogs will enjoy a game of retrieving sticks thrown by their owners. However, this is prudently a game for one dog. If you bring in two or more and throw one stick you are likely to promote a fight. There exists also a danger that a stick in one dog's mouth could gouge out the eye of his companion – so be warned.

Kennels

One Staffordshire Bull Terrier is better kept in the house. He will thrive better in the family circle and because he learns quickly to love his people and home he will usually make a better guard. A dog kept out of doors is not much use to anyone. He becomes bored, often lacks affinity with his owner and is quite capable of ignoring any intruder. Sometimes a Stafford takes fair time to develop his instincts as a guard dog – it is not unusual for a dog to reach eighteen months, even two years of age before he sits up and takes notice of odd happenings. An owner should not be too impatient for the dog will soon learn to give warning barks when necessary. Again, a dog kept out of doors in solitary confinement suffers in the development of his intelligence, whereas the indoor dog seems to know everything that is said to him! However, when a number of dogs are kept the situation is different. Kennel life becomes essential, and there are a number of comfortable models in pre-fabricated kennels to be bought these days from mail order and local sources.

Great care must be taken to pick the right site for the structure and to ensure that it will prove a comfortable and happy home for the dogs, allowing strict hygiene. The kennel site should not be erected under trees, although a screen of trees protecting it from the prevailing winds of the locality is often to be desired. It should stand on well-drained sandy soil or gravel, preferably facing south or south-west. A range of four adjoining kennels is a nice start for the novice with a compartment at one end to house brushes, brooms, shovel, sawdust and disinfectant supplies with easy access. The cautious breeder might well consider a further single kennel placed well away from the rest to be used as a sick bay in emergency.

Many kennels are insufficiently high. This means that the breeder has to spend his time in them in a hunched-up position, which is neither good for the back nor for good kennel hygiene and efficiency. It is best to allow at least six feet from floor to roof so that most people can stand inside with some comfort. Each resident Staffordshire Bull Terrier should have a floor area of about three square metres (9ft^2), at least. If the kennel is to be heated, then allow the dog as much room as possible. With no heating installed, then too much individual space is not such a good thing in winter for the Stafford may be hard put to it to radiate enough body warmth to keep himself cosy. There should be a run of at least 2½ metres (8ft) long to every kennel, bounded on both sides and front by a 3 metres (10ft) high chain link fence. Some Staffordshires are excellent jumpers, so to avoid escapes and accidents it will be best if the run can be topped with chain-link or netting or a perspex roof.

The do-it-yourself kennel builder will be able to produce a lot of refinements and ideas to fit his particular needs, no doubt. However, he will be well advised to study a few professional designs before embarking on his own structure. Draught is a known killer and care must be taken that it cannot penetrate the kennel and debilitate the inmates. The sleeping benches should be made to slide out easily and for simple cleaning. It is also a good idea to improvise a ventilation system which can be adjusted to suit outside weather conditions.

Always try, if finance permits, to construct doors from the run into the outside world on the 'inner chamber' system. This means two doors in use – the outside one you open to enter, then close it with yourself inside. You then open the second door to enter the actual run, safe in the knowledge that the dog within cannot slip past you and escape. Kennel hygiene is vital and this should receive daily attention, going into every corner with a mild, then a stronger, solution for swabbing down the outside concrete runs. 'Dettol' is a well-tried and trusted antiseptic germicide for this job, not only that, but it can be used for bathing cuts, bites, abrasions and stings when prepared in the form of a suitable solution.

An alternative form of run covering to concrete, which perhaps is inclined to retain excess moisture after rain and hold the heat in summer, is prepared with a foundation of coarse clinker topped with a layer of gravel or screened clinker. The whole should be well firmed and most important it should be set over well-drained ground.

6 Exhibiting

Not many people enter the dog show 'game' of their own volition. They are frequently coerced into making an entry at the local canine society's event by some person, who, seeing them with an attractive Staffordshire Bull Terrier, accosts them and informs them that the specimen is a good one and ought to be shown. Most owners are naturally proud of their pedigree Staffords and it takes very little encouragement as a rule to persuade them to try their luck. Knowing next to nothing about the finer points of the breed, let alone the official breed Standard, they hope merely that the dog will win a prize, in much the same way as their attitude would be about buying a raffle ticket! On the other hand, they will not care much if the dog wins nothing, either. In fact, the whole thing is usually treated like a game – which of course, it is at this stage of their interest. Unfortunately, at times, a different aspect arises – their dog, either by virtue of the fact that it has no or only poor competition at the show, wins a major prize. Perhaps other Stafford people present flatter the dog and his owner becomes over-ambitious for him. At times like this there is a danger that the dog-show 'bug' will bite hard and then a simple recreation of exhibiting can become less of a pastime and more of a business, highly competitive and fraught with rivalry and jealousy.

Let it be said at once that dog-showing is a good hobby. It is the shop window of the dog world and develops a keen and healthy competitive spirit among its devotees. To some, concerned largely with the commercial potentialities of the Stafford world, it opens up lucrative possibilities, for the breed is in great demand and produces good prices at home and abroad. Most people who start exhibiting, however, are more concerned with getting expert opinion from the judges on their dogs. Later, they will wish to breed from their bitches, hoping to produce better Staffordshire Bull Terriers in their litters and perhaps be lucky enough to produce a home-bred champion. Also, they will strive for premier show awards to improve, even perpetuate their kennel names. Certainly, in the course of their career they will meet a lot of nice people, make some real and lasting friends and enjoy the social side which exists so warmly in dogdom.

Picking the show

Both the weekly journals devoted to dogs, *Dog World* and *Our Dogs*, maintain show announcement columns. Here the intending exhibitor will find details of shows to be held in the near future. The various types of shows, i.e. Exemption, Sanction, Limited, Open and Championship events, will be represented and once a year the great Kennel Club Cruft's show will be announced in plenty of time for eligible exhibitors to make their plans. All these will offer a good selection for the enthusiast. The procedure is to write or telephone the honorary secretary or show manager of the society concerned and request a schedule of the classification offered. The show might be for Staffordshire Bull Terriers only, in which case it would be termed a Special Breed Club event, alternatively, if many different breeds are classified, it would perhaps be called an All Breeds or Any Variety event.

Both types of shows have their useful features, although it is probably best to enter at shows where only Staffords make the competition. Such a show would be run by one of the specialist societies, a list of these being published at the end of this book, and the judge appointed would be a Staffordshire Bull Terrier expert. This means that every Staffordshire would be judged competently by a specialist and one would possibly get a more detailed opinion of an exhibit from such a person. In any case, all such shows should receive support, particularly from breed lovers, for that helps to keep these shows maintained. It is wise also to show the dog under a number of experienced all-rounder judges in order to test his ability to win in any type of competition.

Types of shows

EXEMPTION SHOWS

The Kennel Club licenses a number of different kinds of dog shows. The most 'junior' form is the Exemption Show. A dog can be entered at such a show even if not registered at the Kennel Club. Neither do the usual Kennel Club rules apply, except that most of the disciplinary rules have to be observed. For pedigree dogs only four classes are permitted where they can be judged according to their various breed points and standards. Such classes have to be of a general nature; 'Any Variety Sporting' and 'Any Variety Open' being two examples. It is usual and popular to arrange the remaining classes so that pedigree dogs, cross-breeds and mongrels can compete against each other. These appear as novelty classes such as 'Dog with the Longest Tail', 'Dog the Judge would like to take Home', 'Dog in Best Condition', 'Dog with the Most Appealing Eyes' and so on. For such shows, the Kennel Club does not specify any special entry fee or prize money, neither does it ask for report on the results and awards. Prize cards throughout are white with black printing, unlike the usual show prize cards which have to be red for first, blue for second and yellow for third. Exemption shows must not be run

Jack McNeil with Ch.
Eastbury Lass (1951).

in conjunction with any registered Canine Society or Training Club, but the officers of such associations may organise or help to run them. Sometimes obedience tests of a simple nature can be incorporated too, but these do not have to be similar to Kennel Club Obedience Tests. Exemption Shows are usually held in aid of charity, often on Bank Holidays.

LIMITED SHOWS
These are shows held under Kennel Club Rules and Regulations, so-called because entry is limited to a certain number of classes and restricted to members of clubs and societies, or to exhibitors within a specified radius or otherwise. Challenge Certificate winners are ineligible at Limited Shows. This type of show is unbenched.

SANCTION SHOWS
This show is also unbenched. It is confined to members of the club or society which is running the show and no Challenge Certificate winners are eligible. No class higher than Post-Graduate may be classified and only twenty classes are permitted when there is more than one breed or variety. When only one breed, such as the Staffordshire Bull Terrier, is concerned, the show must not comprise more than ten classes.

OPEN SHOWS

Such shows can be benched or otherwise. Very often they are held in conjunction with an Agricultural Show. No restrictions are made as to exhibitors making entries in the classes provided; conditions being similar to those at a championship show, but without provision of Challenge Certificates.

CHAMPIONSHIP SHOWS

These are the most important shows and are really Open Shows held under the rules and regulations of the Kennel Club at which Challenge Certificates are offered and may be competed for. Some of the all-breed shows can occupy one, two or even three days; the specialist shows, i.e. shows at which one breed such as the Staffordshire Bull Terrier might appear, are one-day events. Cruft's Dog Show, the most important dog show in the world, caters for almost every variety, offering Challenge Certificates for most and is a three-day event in London.

MATCHES

These are not dog shows in the strict sense of the words, but must not escape mention for they are popular among doggy people. They are conducted under Kennel Club rules and regulations, and are competitions on the familiar knock-out system between pairs of dogs, a prize of

Cruft's Dog Show 1939: (*left to right*) F. Roberts with Coronation Scot, Harry Melling with Tough Guy, H. N. Beilby with Mrs M. Beare's Ch. Midnight Gift, Joe Dunn with Ch. Lady Eve, Joe Mallen with Ch. Gentleman Jim and Judge, Harry Pegg (*standing*).

some description being awarded to the final winner – Best Dog in Match. Clubs usually run these shows for member-education, either between dogs owned by club members or in challenge with dogs belonging to members of rival clubs, either with the same breed or different.

Show preparations

TRAINING FOR SHOW

The first thing a show dog must learn is to be handled. This entails standing still while the judge goes over him from nose to tail, feeling, prodding, pushing and shifting all the time. This is how the judge will learn the extent of his development, his structure and soundness. He must get used to having his lips lifted for examination of the teeth; his private parts handled to ensure that he is entire and his forefeet lifted for feet inspection. A lot of dogs object to such things and those who do seldom get far in the show awards, for the judge quite rightly concurs that a dog who cannot be handled and assessed, cannot be judged.

Ch. Karjobri Black Pepper, owned by Mr and Mrs B. Grattridge.

It is advisable, therefore, that when a promising puppy is about to try his luck in the show ring that he should make his début fully trained in this performance and know how to accept it with good grace. An ideal plan is to go through the typical actions of a judge with him at every opportunity. Ask your friends to do the same when they visit you. Strangers too should be invited to run their hands over him at every opportunity, so that he gets used to the handling routine and does not flinch from it. A lucky owner is he who owns a good puppy which proves to be a natural showman. This is a dog which does not seem to care how roughly he is pummelled by a judge and enjoys every minute of the show, acts in an orderly fashion and even seems to preen when being exhibited. Given a dog like this – a canine extrovert – there is no need to worry for half the battle is won. However, most dogs can, with patience, be trained to perform well, and good show prospect is worth a few hours' training every week.

The best time to start a puppy on his show training course is just before his meal. The best place to do it is somewhere nice and quiet, away from all distractions in a spare room or in the garden at home. If he has had already some of the elementary training discussed, he will have learned already the pleasures of doing what he is told and have a good, solid groundwork to offer for this new phase of instruction. He should be on his lead at all times during this course, just as you would have him in the show ring. Try him standing to see if he has a natural stance, i.e. without human assistance. Occasionally, a dog has this and it is preferable to a position into which he has been encouraged by manual placing. If he is structurally sound and typical with good balance when standing, it is likely that he will be able to 'show himself', that is, fall into a pleasing and attractive pose. However, if he really needs placing by hand, make sure that the way you put him or 'mould' him into place is correct and that it displays his good points to advantage while minimising the faults.

Care should be taken not to spread him too wide in front. The Staffordshire Bull Terrier's legs should be straight and parallel with each other down to the wrists (pasterns) where they turn out a little. If you put the palm of your right hand between his legs and under his chest, then lift him slightly off the ground, allowing him to regain the floor naturally, then a good position should be obtained. Check on the forelegs when viewed from the side. They should run vertically from shoulders to ground. The front feet should be parallel with the rear feet too, and to show the position of the feet better, each foot should appear in the four corners of an imaginary rectangle when viewed from above. Note however, that the Staffordshire Bull Terrier hind stance carries considerable importance with most judges. Its angulation requires well-bent stifles (there are a lot of straight stifles in the breed today, unfortunately). The hind feet must not, therefore, be allowed in a position too far forward or too much under the dog. Note too that the feet of the hind limbs should not stretch out too far the other way or it will look as though the dog is sliding forward into a collapse! A study should be made of successful show winners and good Staffordshire Bull Terrier photographs to determine this point and when assessed properly, then emulated. As soon as the required position has been found and the dog placed in it, the command 'Stand!' should be given. Every time the dog is put down into place the command should be repeated. No doubt he will fidget at first, but with encouragement and the usual titbit reward for co-operative behaviour he will soon learn to 'stay put' and eventually stand firm in his position even when handled. A danger exists, with manual placing of this kind that the exhibit will appear 'wooden'. He need not if his attention is maintained and livened with the anticipation of a titbit from his owner's hand. In any case, when he gets into the show ring there will be plenty of interesting dogs and objects to attract him and, more important, to keep him on his toes.

A puppy being trained in this way should not have more than a ten-minute lesson at a time. Youngsters get bored quickly and soon go stale with continual instruction. This has to be avoided or progress will be retarded. The time is now ripe for the puppy to show how well he can stand with distractions around him. Up to now he has done very well in some quiet nook, but he will find the show ring a very noisy and busy place with more dogs together than he has ever seen before – quite apart from people! He must be taken, therefore, to a room or place where many distractions exist. A good idea to condition him to such a situation is to join the local dog-training club. Most of these bodies have their meetings in nearby halls and cost little to join. Here, the puppy can be taken and get not only the dog-show atmosphere he needs to prepare him for his début at a real show, but expert advice and prompting in the important matters of deportment and posture. Here too, you will be able to deploy him around a ring or up and down so that he gets used to moving a typical distance up to and away from a presiding judge when the time comes for a proper show. An effective way to get him to turn well in this movement is to give a sharp snap of the fingers as you drag on the lead to achieve a smart turn about face. Do this consistently with the lead drag until you find he will do the turn as he hears the snap, no lead pressure being needed.

The pupil must be taught to move at a speed which suits him. At this correct speed he will show his good points to advantage while minimising the effect of his faults. A dog moved too fast or too slow will almost certainly achieve an unfavourable aspect in the ring. The proper Staffordshire Bull Terrier gait is an individual one, treading neither wide nor narrow with his front feet; the limbs of the hindquarters showing some degree of parallelism when going away and with ample, spring, stride and rhythm. The action in all limbs has to be positive, neither weaving, ambling, fleeting, 'paddling' or high-stepping. Such styles of action are perhaps desirable in some other breeds, but not in the Staffordshire. In this breed, obliquely set shoulders and well-let-down hocks are standard equipment and any specimen which is loose in shoulders, out at elbows or with upright shoulders and high hocks, cannot move in a typical manner.

To produce good movement in the breed, it is necessary to fix both the structural details and pre-disposing nervous qualities genetically when breeding. When showing, good selection and discrimination by a breeder should be evident in the exhibit's action. It stands to reason that a dog when pulling or scrambling on his lead will have his head thrust forward, his shoulders thrown out sideways and his fore-action impossible to assess. Alternatively, if he moves sluggishly, the beautiful and rhythmic muscular co-ordination we expect from the hindquarters of a moving Staffordshire Bull Terrier is lost.

Teach the dog to make the best of himself at all times; it is just as important too that you remain aware of his good ring behaviour from the moment you enter the ring with him to the time you leave. If you relax for just one second, this might be the very moment when the judge turns on his heel to consider you for a prime placing. If your exhibit looks jaded and is sitting on his haunches instead of looking alert and up on his toes, then he doesn't deserve the prize he might have got. Ringcraft is an exhibitor's science. It needs to be studied with care and applied with skill. Others might have dogs as good as, even better perhaps, than yours, but with your extra knowledge of this way to make the best of your Stafford, even to disguise his faults, your chances of beating them are enhanced.

7 Diseases, Ailments and Conditions

The average Staffordshire Bull Terrier lives about ten and a half years. Being evolved originally from the Bulldog (a comparatively short-lived breed) and a Terrier (among the longest-lived canines), his expectation of life, barring accidents, falls somewhere between the two. Examples of Staffords living to, and beyond, fifteen years of age have been quoted, but such cases are rare. Age in an adult dog is difficult to determine. Once the dog has left the puppy stage, when the teeth can offer some indication of the animal's age, it is not possible to verify age without authentic pedigree. Most dogs retain their faculties up to ten years of age and an owner should not expect a working or sporting dog to go through a hard day after that age. In the show world a dog is considered a Veteran from the age of seven years and it is not uncommon for Staffordshire Bull Terrier stud dogs to sire excellent litters at ten or even twelve years of age; in fact, some breeders believe their best litters come from dogs of advanced years. On the female side, bitches of ten years of age, even more, have been known to produce litters, but it is to be hoped that these were the results of accidental matings rather than contrived unions. It is considered that six years of age is the maximum age at which a Staffordshire Bull Terrier bitch should be allowed a litter.

Staffordshires, generally, are dogs which keep reasonably fit, but not many go through their lives without experiencing at least some sickness or disease which requires nursing at home. Clearly, a book of this category is unable to engage professionally in the subject of veterinary medicine. However, the commoner ailments are dealt with in simple form to give the inexperienced owner some guidance as to maintaining his dog in good health and to care for him in the most effective way when he is sick. The best investment against illness is good rearing from puppyhood, nutritive feeding and conditioning with ample exercise, intelligent maintenance and control.

A good dog is worth all the good things one can put into him, but more important, he *must* be immunised against the serious virus diseases which scourge dogs. These include Distemper, Hard-Pad, Hepatitis, Parvo-virus (which has appeared only in recent years) and the bacterial jaundice inducing a disease known as Leptospirosis, which is contracted from the urine of rats. The first two diseases are far less menacing than they used to be, due to modern vaccine techniques, but they, like the others, need preventive action by the dog owner. Leptospirosis in both its forms has been well under control for some time and Hepatitis, a liver disease, is much better controlled than it used to be. Parvo-virus, however, is still taking its toll of dogs and an effective immuniser in the form of feline live enteritis vaccine is in use against this 'cat-flu' type of virus. All such vaccines should be inoculated only by the qualified veterinarian. If one resides outside Great Britain it is as well to discuss these safeguards with a competent authority as sometimes vaccines vary in their form and effect, especially in hot countries.

These virus afflictions are discussed briefly in the following pages as are other diseases, ailments and conditions which trouble the dog.

Infectious and contagious diseases

DISTEMPER

One of the earliest known canine diseases, the dog being most open to it when between the ages of three and eighteen months, although it can be caught anytime. Modern veterinary medicine seems to have mastered its effects which include pneumonia, enteritis symptoms and so on, but the worst part of it in patients seemingly cured is the aftermath of Chorea, etc., nervous disorders which can seldom if ever, be corrected.

The symptoms usually noted with the oncoming of viral infection are loss of appetite, diarrhoea, possibly vomiting and some swelling of the neck glands. The owner should take the patient's temperature and any reading over 38.8°C (102°F) should be the signal to get veterinary advice. The dog will want to sleep more than normal, possibly his eyes will become bloodshot and a dry cough will be noted. Feeding should be cut down drastically, boiled water and honey being recommended to allay increased fever. It is not unusual for a sufferer to have little fits, but these should pass with the curing of the disease.

The usual time to have a dog injected with vaccine against Distemper is at three months of age, although some proprietary vaccines are claimed effective at around two months of age. Immunity is reasonably secure, but it is advisable to have 'booster' inoculations at recommended intervals. These will give continued protection.

HARD-PAD

This appears a close relative in the virus field to Distemper, but is a harsher disease and more distressing, also more serious. It is really a form of Encephalitis, consequently it needs immediate treatment, although in its early stages it might be confused with Distemper as the symptoms are similar, and in fact initial treatment is as for that disease. Occasionally, the Hard-Pad victim will become encrusted around the eyes and nostrils and the pads of the feet will swell and harden. The veterinary surgeon will know how to deal with this disease, which can prove fatal.

HEPATITIS

Canine Virus Hepatitis or Rubarth's Disease. Highly infectious, it can prove a speedy killer, although a dog which has managed to survive five days will often pull through. The virus attacks the liver and blood vessels, jaundice being an unpleasant symptom, also a temperature of up to 40°C (104°F), with abnormal sleepiness, no appetite, diarrhoea and vomiting. Bitches with this disease have been afterwards affected adversely in their productive powers and the ever increasing incidence of 'fading' puppies has been attributed to the effect of this disease. The vaccine used is one which acts jointly against the virus with Distemper and Hard-Pad.

PARVO-VIRUS

When this disease erupted in dogdom, it was diagnosed as a form of cat-flu and it was treated as such, with vaccines evolved from feline dead enteritis later to be replaced with feline live enteritis embodiments. The virus appears a difficult one to combat and veterinary circles are watching the progress of their vaccines with some concern at the present time.

LEPTOSPIROSIS

Two forms of this disease are encountered, one being Leptospiral Jaundice (*L. icterrohaemorrhagia*), the other *L. canicola*. The former attacks the liver and is contracted from the urine of rats. This causes jaundice and internal haemorrhage and is obviously very dangerous. The latter attacks the kidneys, the infection coming from the urine of an infected dog. It is the less virulent of the two varieties of bacteria, but although a dog might seemingly be cured after just a few days of fever and depression, it is believed that some damage might affect his kidneys, proving fatal in later life. It is almost impossible for the layman to differentiate between the two forms, diagnosis and specialised treatment being the job of the veterinary surgeon. Vaccination covers both types, a further injection being given after a fortnight. Every effort should be made to eliminate rats in the area if they are suspected and strict hygiene in the kennel is essential, especially as it is thought a dog can be a carrier for the disease through his urine for some time after being cured.

While on the subject of diseases which attack the dog, mention should be made of two more which might be encountered.

COCCIDIOSIS

This is a highly infectious disease requiring strict kennel hygiene as it is contracted from stools, in which the spore forms of the parasite exist. The parasite itself is not unlike the one which attacks poultry and the affected dog will sicken and lose weight quickly. Blood-spattered diarrhoea is a typical symptom and this bowel disorder needs early correction by taking the dog off raw meat and concentrating on milky feeds meanwhile.

TETANUS

This is contracted through open wounds. Known as 'Lockjaw', the germs produce a nerve-paralysing poison, with resultant stiffness and muscle spasm. It is not commonly reported in dogs, but care should be taken to treat deep wounds according to their form and arrange with the veterinary surgeon to inject with anti-tetanus specific as a safeguard. The patient should be confined to a dark room and put on to a simple menu.

Minor ailments

ABSCESS

This is a localised collection of pus and matter under a swelling of skin, which has a shiny appearance. With the aid of hot fomentations and gentle pressure it can be made to burst and the pus disposed. Then dress the open wound with 'TCP' or similar preparation dabbed on with a wad of clean cotton wool. When draining the pus away make sure it is done from the lowest point of the abscess when the dog is standing naturally. If normal efforts fail to clear it, it may be necessary to gently pierce the swelling with the point of a sterilised needle; better still, ask the veterinary surgeon to call.

Regular daily attention is required when dealing with an abscess and it is important to ensure that the wound does not close before all the pus has been removed, so after each squeezing, pack the hole with antiseptic ointment and remember that the abscess must heal from within and not from just the closure of the wound. The place should be examined at frequent intervals until it has healed.

ACCIDENT

If the Staffordshire Bull Terrier has been run over, keep him quiet, treating for shock. Internal injury may be indicated by bloodless gums. Keep the patient warm with blankets, soothing him meanwhile with the voice and hands until the veterinary surgeon arrives.

ACNE

This is inflammation of the skin follicles, causing an eruption of pimples, which eventually break and emit pus, later drying to form scabs. It is usually found on the dog's under-belly and in the area of the stop. It is irritating, and with constant scratching the dog can become distressed. Veterinary advice should be sought, but home treatment entails dusting the acne with medicinal powder after moistening the area with witch-hazel.

ANAL GLANDS

These two small glands are situated one on either side of the anus entrance. In early wild life of the dog they held a foul fluid which the animal would eject at will to make a trail. Domesticity has caused these glands to fall into disuse and they are inclined to clog with waste matter, become chafed and cause distress and discomfort. Signs of this irritation will often be given when the animal rubs his rear along the ground or turns round suddenly to attempt a nibble at his rear parts. The offending matter can be squeezed out simply enough by taking a palm-sized pad of clean cotton wool in the hand, lift up the dog's tail and press the wad hard against the anus, squeezing and kneading the glands. This area should have regular and adequate attention; failure to give attention could easily result in abscesses.

ANAL (AND RECTAL) PROLAPSIS

Common in puppies, occasionally in older dogs. It can be caused by worm infection or straining due to constipation. Whereas the prolapsis can be replaced by the veterinary surgeon under anaesthetic, the *cause* of the straining should be removed without delay.

ANAL TUMOURS

These are usually found in older dogs, arising from small rectal glands. A veterinary surgeon can easily deal with these and there is no reason why they should reappear.

APPETITE, LACK OF

This is usual in worm-infected puppies: it is also a danger signal symptom of the more serious virus infections. The possibility of such infection should be considered if the puppy's temperature is found to be abnormal. In ordinary circumstances, appetite may be improved with a change of diet.

APPETITE, PERVERTED

Puppies and occasionally older dogs, especially bitches, have the unpleasant habit of eating coke, stones, even their own and other dogs' stools. The cause is probably some dietetic deficiency and as dogs are natural scavengers, it should not unduly worry the owner. Providing the intake of such things as coal is not excessive, the charcoal additives involved will do good, but it will be as well to revise the animal's diet and step up raw meat feeding with extra vitamins and minerals.

ASTHMA

Fat and overweight dogs usually experience this distressing complaint. The symptoms noted are short, dry coughs, shortage of breath and snuzzly breathing. The first thing to do is get down the animal's weight, give more raw meat in the diet and avoid taxing the heart with heavy exercise.

BAD BREATH

Commonly caused by excess of tartar on and behind the teeth, or ulceration which has been induced by moisture encrusting in the folds and wrinkles of the face, especially in the case of an elderly dog. When Halitosis is unbearable, action on the teeth and ulceration must be drastic. However, mild cases can be rectified by giving the dog something hard like a marrow bone or biscuit to chew. A weak solution of hydrogen peroxide, applied to the ulceration with a pad of cotton wool will be found effective. The tartar must be scraped away carefully with a special tool available for the purpose.

BALANITIS

A discharge from the male dog's penis, seldom found in a dog at regular stud. A mild solution of antiseptic such as 'TCP' diluted 1:5 in tepid water should be syringed gently beneath the sheath morning and night until the condition is dispersed. These discharges are seldom of long duration.

BALDNESS

Often caused by nervous debility, poor condition or glandular thyroid disorder. The diet should be totally revised, ensuring a greater raw meat intake and regular exercise. Synonymous with Alopaecia.

BEE STINGS

Apply 'TCP' or similar antiseptic neat directly to the stings. Give little aspirin to ease pain and treat for shock, as required. If stinging is extensive call the veterinary surgeon.

BILIOUS ATTACK

First signs are usually nausea and vomiting. The dog's temperature should be recorded to ensure that these are not symptoms of something more serious. Be warned by sub-normal or abnormal readings of one degree only and if worried call the veterinary surgeon. Take away solid food and give mixture of white of egg, one teaspoonful of glucose with tablespoonful of boiled water, the whole well beaten. A few drops of brandy can be usefully added. Dosage: one teaspoonful every hour. Keep patient warm and in dark.

BITES

ANIMAL: Antiseptic solution from 'TCP' or Iodine should be dripped into the wound with a pipette or similar dropper, *after* the wound area has been shaved and cleaned. Bad bites should be referred at once to the veterinary surgeon.

SNAKE: The veterinary surgeon should be called at once. First Aid include application of a tourniquet above the bite if it is on foot or leg. Emergency treatment would include cutting a deep 'X' over the bite or fang marks and dripping potassium-permanganate into the wound so made.

BLADDER

INFLAMMATION OF: If the dog can be persuaded to drink large quantities of water or milk it will help to flush out the system and cure the condition, which is one of Cystitis and inclined to persist. The cause can be due to a house-trained dog, habitually clean, forced to hold himself for extended periods. This will result in the bladder becoming distended and inflamed with a rise in body temperature and loss of appetite. Such a condition is for the veterinary surgeon to deal with.

STONES IN: If a dog's urine, which is acid, is neutralised or becomes alkaline, a sediment is left in the bladder which contributes to the making of small stones, some of which can get lodged in the urethra and cause a blockage. Surgical treatment is necessary, but a consistent raw meat diet helps a lot to prevent such conditions.

WEAKNESS: Usually experienced by older dogs unable to hold themselves for very long, or with the bitch in whelp whose forward puppies are pressing on her bladder, making it impossible for her to be continent. Such animals, being normally clean in their habits, become worried at their lapses. This is where the owner can allay their worries by refraining from scolding and showing understanding. The floor of the sleeping quarters should be lined with newspapers or a sand and dirt box provided. These can be disposed of every morning without fuss and the system kept until the animals have reverted to their normal clean habits or have been reassured. Sometimes bladder weaknesses indicate kidney disorder, which needs professional veterinary attention.

BLINDNESS

All puppies are born blind, this being Nature's way of protecting them during the first few days of their lives. Until they are nine or ten days old, when they see some daylight, they are unlikely to wander or suffer eye damage. Congenital blindness is quite another matter and rare in the Staffordshire Bull Terrier. It is known as Progressive Retinal Atrophy (PRA for short) and is hereditary. This can be eradicated only through selective breeding. (See also Cataracts.)

BOWEL

INFECTION: Enteritis, the most common result of infection, must be treated immediately. It starts off usually with simple diarrhoea which if unattended can deteriorate into a dark, sometimes blood-splattered and unpleasant stool. If allowed to progress further, the animal will become prostrate. The cause must be determined and dealt with as advised by the veterinary surgeon, but initial action is to withdraw all meat feeding and give only milky foods.

BLOCKAGE: Purgatives seldom prove effective in dislodging internal obstructions. Veterinary help must be obtained either to diagnose the trouble, such as a tumour or to remove it by surgery.

BRONCHITIS

A chill might well prove the forerunner of this debilitating complaint. Draughts and failure to rub down a dog after a swim or walk in the rain have been known to cause it. The temperature should be taken; bronchitis usually shows up at between 39° and 40°C (103° and 104°F). The patient will need warmth, yet plenty of air movement around him and light feeding such as steamed white fish, gruel and chicken, etc. is indicated. The sometimes severe dry coughing which accompanies this complaint can be alleviated by nasal drops given under veterinary supervision. Some breeders keep a Bronchitis Kennel for such cases. This can be an ordinary box like a tea-chest or travelling box, with a small hole in it through which the spout of a kettle can be directed. A measure of Friar's Balsam or similar can be mixed with the water in the kettle; this should be boiled and the vapour directed through to the dog in the box. Three or four times a day this should be repeated ten minutes at a time until improvement has been noted.

BRUISES

It is seldom possible to see a bruise on a dog without close inspection, his coat hiding a good deal. However, it is obvious that if the animal has been hit by a car, or has cuts and wounds caused by some heavy blow, then bruising exists. Any open wounds or abrasions must be dealt with and bathed with warm water into which a few drops of reliable antiseptic have been poured. Bed with a hot water bottle will do much to relieve local pain and boiled water into which honey has been added makes an advisable feed in the initial stages. Care must be taken with older dogs especially, that the bruising is completely dispersed. If treated casually, permanent stiffness can ensue and aged animals require a lot of reassurance and understanding from their owners at such a time.

BURNS AND SCALDS
Burns produce dry heat injuries, whereas scalds are moist heat effects. The same treatment can be directed to both forms, but first treat for shock and keep the patient quiet, giving him a teaspoonful of bicarbonate of soda followed by as much fluid in the form of warm milk and glucose as he will take. Bicarbonate of soda should also be applied to the affected area in pack form after removing any impeding coat. The mixture should be in the form of 1 oz to 1 pt of boiled water, and soaked into a pad which will adequately cover the wound. After effects of burns and scalds are frequently severe. Great care should be taken to ensure that infection is kept at bay and diet should be as nutritive as possible, with ample protein such as raw meat to build up the patient once he is convalescent. Never use oils or ointments for treatment as these are capable of generating heat. Treat also for shock (see Collapse) as this is present in all burned or scalded dogs.

CANCER
A progressive, often malignant tumour which destroys the tissues where it grows. Any lump or swelling noted on the dog should be referred to the veterinary surgeon as early treatment may prove successful.

CANKER (OF THE EAR)
The affected dog will invariably show his discomfort by holding his head on one side, shaking it and pawing the affected ear. On inspection, it will be found that the ear channel is clogged with a dark brown waxy substance which is hard and emits a pungent odour, which is most unpleasant. Treatment must be given at once and properly applied the condition will be easily corrected. It is always a bit hazardous to use implements in the ear, so far as possible remove some of the hard, waxy lumps with the fingers and thumb. If this proves too difficult, small tweezers should be employed, but with the greatest care, and gentleness. Sometimes the ear will be found discharging and this will mean it will have to be dried out with small pieces of cotton wool which are securely wrapped round a wooden cocktail stick from which the point has been severed, but only if it is not possible to succeed with the fingers. A useful remedy is 'Otosporin', two drops of this being inserted down the ear channel twice a day for three days, then massaged well in, but the ear must be dry before this is done, also cleaned out thoroughly. On the fourth day, clean the ear, as usual, and lower a ¼-teaspoonsful of Boracic powder into the channel. Do this twice a day until the canker has

disappeared. If the patient seems disturbed and is in pain, an aspirin should be given just before he retires. It should be part of the regular grooming to check up on the patient's ears. In this way, no abnormal condition is allowed to progress to become chronic.

CATARACTS

This is opacity of the lens and can occur in both eyes. It is met occasionally in older Staffordshire Bull Terriers when vision is seriously impaired. Surgery can be employed with hope of moderate success, but it is a progressive condition and not a great deal seems to be known about it as far as dogs are concerned, probably because serious eye conditions are difficult to treat in animals.

Most specimens noted by the author have been fawns, of roughly similar physical appearance and type, most with some protuberance of the eyes. Certain individual dogs of a particular line have been pinpointed as passing on the incidence of cataracts, but this is not a conclusive factor. Recent cases of blindness are being examined in the light of modern knowledge of 'PRA' (Progressive Retinal Atrophy) which has affected some breeds, mostly in the sporting section.

CAT BITES

Cat bites and scratches are dangerous in that they are frequently germladen, the bites particularly being deep and inaccessible. The bitten area should be shaved and bathed with 'TCP' and the prudent owner would arrange for his dog to receive an anti-tetanus, or similar injection.

CHOKING

Death can quickly result from any obstruction in a dog's throat. Asphyxiation can be prevented by trying to hook it out with the forefinger, providing it can be reached. If the object lies back too far the best thing is to push it further down. Two people are best to cope with an incident like this; one to force open the dog's jaws, the other to probe for the obstruction. The chances of getting bitten in the process have to be weighed against the dog's life being saved. Many such affairs can be prevented by making sure he does not play with objects like rubber toys, small bones and chunks of wood without supervision. Watch too for oversize and gristly lumps of meat in his food, for these are main perils.

CHOREA: (See: Distemper.)

CLEFT PALATE

This is where the hard roof of the dog's mouth is cleft instead of being flat. A congenital fault, it causes the animal to blow out through the nostrils the milk he suckles through the mouth, due to no vacuum being formed in the mouth. Such unfortunate puppies are better painlessly destroyed as surgery is not successful.

COLIC

An advanced form of indigestion which can cause the dog great discomfort. Warmth and local massage will usually put right the matter, but when attacks persist dose the Stafford with one teaspoonful of ordinary bicarbonate of soda.

COLITIS

A painful and often difficult condition to treat. The larger bowel is inflamed and diarrhoea and anaemic effects are noted symptoms. Nursing entails rest, reassurance and light diet.

COLLAPSE

This resembles shock and treatment must be given accordingly. It can be caused following an accident on the road or a fight, or even due to a heart condition. The temperature when taken will be found on the low side and breathing is shallow. Lay the dog on his right side, raise the hindquarters, keeping the head low. If he is *conscious* and seems able to swallow put a few drops of brandy on the back of his tongue. Never give anything orally to an unconscious patient. The veterinary surgeon must be called in such cases.

CONSTIPATION

This is frequently caused by too much starchy food such as biscuit meal in excess of raw meat, etc. However, the cause must first be explored for bowel stoppages must not be discounted if the condition persists. Exercise should be increased with general toning up and the dog's diet must be improved at once. To cope with ordinary constipation there are a number of good proprietary laxatives on the market. Chronic cases should be referred to the veterinary surgeon.

CONCUSSION

Normally brought about by a heavy blow on the head. The dog should be kept warm in a darkened room and a stone hot water bottle put in his bed and covered with an old sock or similar. Call the veterinary surgeon, but first aid can be rendered by applying cold compresses to the head. The dog should not be dosed through the mouth.

CYSTS

These can spring up on the dog's back, in fact on any part of his body, but they appear more commonly as interdigital cysts. They prove painful and the dog is usually rendered lame, for the cysts are like small boils.

Dipping the dog's feet into warm water or applying a few poultices will often bring the cysts to bursting point, when they should be bathed with a weak antiseptic solution. Persistent cysts may require surgical treatment, but a *complete* change of diet is recommended before resorting to this, a trial diet of from three to four weeks being best.

CYSTITIS (See: Bladder Infection.)

CUTS

The cuts should be bathed over carefully with warm water to assess their severity. If the wound extends beyond one inch, it may require suturing by the veterinary surgeon. The surface of the cut should be protected with lint and bandage meanwhile and the 'lips' of the wound should be compressed together to hasten healing.

DANDRUFF

Dogs occasionally develop dandruff, since the skin, like that of humans, continually sheds and renews itself. Regular brushing and grooming will obviate this.

DEAFNESS

Not met with in Staffordshire Bull Terriers, as far as author is aware. Not uncommon years ago in White English Bull Terrier, but harsh selective remedies used to breed out this congenital fault and in these days no evidence of deafness in that breed exists. The author has never encountered a congenitally deaf Staffordshire Bull Terrier, even an all-white which some might consider prone to the trouble. A puppy does not hear until it is at least three weeks of age, relying upon vibrations caused by movement or encounter for warning. Consequently, it is not easy to assess deafness in whelps when they are so young. Various experiments can be made such as rattling a feeding dish when all the puppies are asleep; keeping close watch on the reactions of the individuals. A puppy suffering from deafness would be slow to react and deafness might then be suspected.

DEMODECTIC MANGE

This is sometimes known as 'red' mange, due to the reddening of the affected parts. It causes intense discomfort with some thickening of the tissue. The patient loses appetite and condition and the veterinary surgeon should advise treatment for this is not easily cured.

DERMATITIS

This takes the form of an eczema with red and raw suppurating areas which eventually become encrusted. Surrounding hair should be carefully trimmed away, the affected parts dressed with antiseptic and drying remedies which the veterinary surgeon will prescribe.

DIABETES

The dog quickly loses condition, although his appetite is abnormal and he seems to require a lot of liquid. Urine is light in colour and laboratory tests will reveal excessive sugar content. Tiredness and diarrhoea, with possible vomiting, can be expected. He should be put on to raw meat diet with a small pinch of bicarbonate of soda at every meal. Treatment is a matter for the veterinary surgeon.

DIARRHOEA

This is Nature's way of cleansing the body of impurities and waste matter, absorbed in the form of unsuitable food, etc. However, the condition is represented in the pattern of several virus diseases such as Distemper, etc., and when diarrhoea persists unabated for more than two days, in spite of careful treatment, it needs to be viewed very seriously. The first effort should be to harden up the dog's motions. Raw meat feeding should be withdrawn and he should be put entirely on milky meals – bread and warm milk is particularly good in halting transitory diarrhoea. If some increase in temperature is noted, the veterinary surgeon should be called in immediately to ascertain its cause.

DISCHARGES

These need prompt attention, for quite apart from being unpleasant, some form of infection is implied, and the veterinary surgeon should be asked to investigate at once.

DISCHARGE FROM TEATS: (See: Chapter Four. After-whelping Problems/Excess Milk.)

DISCHARGE FROM PENIS: (See: Balanitis.)

DISCHARGE FROM RECTUM: (See: Anal Glands.)

DISCHARGE FROM WOUNDS: If the dog can reach the cut with his tongue, this will prove the best medicine. If he cannot, then the discharge – which is serum oozing from the broken skin – can be dealt with by constant bathing with a weak solution of 'TCP' – allowed as much fresh air as possible and the patient given plenty of exercise.

DISCHARGE FROM VAGINA: This is usually experienced by a bitch after whelping. She will have no appetite and become weaker. It must be checked that she did not retain any afterbirth during her whelping, for this can prove very dangerous and peritonitis can develop, or other septic condition. The veterinary surgeon can inject with Pituitrin to offset this and he should be called in to deal with all abnormal discharges. Occasionally, after a bitch has been mated she will re-commence blood flow from the vagina. This must be examined at once as any disruption of the oestral flow should be viewed with suspicion. Likewise, careful watch should be kept on such a bitch during the gestation of her puppies to ensure normal progress.

DISCHARGE FROM MOUTH: (See: Bad Breath.)

DISCHARGE FROM EYES: The commonest form is conjunctivitis, which is a weeping condition. This can be cleared up quickly enough, using a conventional veterinary product, although it is liable to recur mildly at intervals. However, more serious eye troubles than this exist to worry the dog and his owner and such forms as DISTICHIASIS, ECTROPION and ENTROPION are discussed in this Chapter.

DISCHARGE FROM NOSE: A dog perspires through his nose and it is a sign of good health if there is a constant and clear slight discharge to dampen it. However, if mucus is noted from the nostrils the matter needs urgent attention as this could be the beginning of something serious.

DISLOCATIONS

The commonest dislocation experienced is in the hip joint, toe joints being next in order. An X-ray will be required to determine the degree of dislocation and to ensure there is no fracture. The dog should be laid in as near to a natural position as possible and restrained from movement until the arrival of the veterinary surgeon. If the patient seems anxious and restless, a sedative should be given.

DISTICHIASIS

An unpleasant condition of the eye where a double row of lashes grow on the lids and turn slightly inwards. The eyeball is continually brushed and irritated, causing copious weeping. Surgery can be employed to remove the superfluous lashes; home treatment with a pair of eyebrow tweezers providing little more than temporary relief.

DROWNING

Employ artificial respiration after the dog has been laid on his side. The flat of the hand should push down firmly against the ribs, then lifted sharply, the action being repeated at strict intervals of about eighteen exhalations a minute for a Stafford. It should be noted that it is important to keep the dog's tongue extended from the mouth during treatment. An assistant can sometimes be usefully employed doing this while artificial respiration is applied.

DRY ECZEMA

Another form of Mange. The patches are usually grey, rather like elephant skin to touch and these will become pustular but dry over quickly. The dog will be intensely irritated and scratch and cause further encrustment. Veterinary advice should be sought for the cause.

ECLAMPSIA (See Chapter Four.)

ECTROPION
This is a condition where the eyelids turn slightly outwards failing to give protection to the eyes from dust, pollen, etc. The haw is visibly exposed. The condition can be remedied by surgery.

ECZEMA
This is a skin condition which starting with bare patches becomes pustular and breaks with a discharge which eventually encrusts, causing severe irritation. The hair around the affected area must be trimmed away and the patches dressed with suitable antibiotic dressing, cortisone for example having been found effective. This form of skin disorder is inclined to develop a weeping spread under the scabbing. The veterinary surgeon must be consulted for up-to-date treatment.

ENCEPHALITIS: (See: Hardpad.)

ENTROPION
This is an eye condition where the eyelids turn slightly inwards, usually the lower lids. It is an inherited fault and if not dealt with the eye cornea will be damaged. Correction is a surgical matter.

EPISTAXIS
Nose-bleeding, caused either by a blow on the nose or by foreign bodies in the nasal membranes. If the latter it may prove necessary to get veterinary treatment. If the former, the blood flow can be arrested by applying ice-packs.

EPILEPSY
There appears to be no cure for this. The dog will fall to the ground, twitching, sometimes whimpering. Sedatives can be given and the animal will appear none the worse. Minor fits such as teething convulsions are caused by pain in the gums, but these are a passing phase which can be obviated if the puppy is given a large marrow bone to gnaw and help his teeth come through.

EPULIS
A hard fibrous growth originating at the tooth and gum margins, found mostly in older dogs. It can be removed by surgery.

EYES

The simplest form is Conjunctivitis which can be dealt with at home by careful application of specially prepared eye ointments, obtainable from your veterinary surgeon or from a proprietary supplier. (See also: Disichiasis, Ectropion, Entropion.)

FITS

Puppies often have fits during teething when the second teeth are coming through. It is not serious and the fits are brief. A suitable sedative can be prescribed if you are worried about it and wish confirmation that nothing more serious is entailed. Some fits are the aftermath of Distemper etc., others are of epilectic origin — these need professional veterinary treatment.

GANGRENE

This may follow a neglected wound, or a section of a limb too tightly bound following a fracture. Staffordshires sometimes chase their tails, nipping the ends and drawing blood. Never bind a wound so tightly that circulation is impaired. Be immediately suspicious of skin which has turned black or blue. Gangrene is seen to be well advanced when the part has died and turned green. Needless to say, a veterinary surgeon should be consulted a long time before this occurs.

GASTRO-ENTERITIS

Diarrhoea is the usual symptom and in advanced cases it is often marked with blood, at which stage it is serious. Vomiting is noted and this has the appearance of beaten white of egg. Abdominal pain is evident, but not necessarily any rise in temperature. The dog should be taken off meat and put on to milky foods at once. It is better if he is segregated from his companions too. All such bowel disorders should entail veterinary advice.

GLAUCOMA

This causes enlargement of the eyeball brought about by pressure of fluid inside. It is a hereditary condition and serious therefore.

GRASS SEEDS

The summer months, especially that of July, find brittle, ripe stalks in the fields. These will split and the little florets from the seed heads will penetrate the dog's skin beneath his coat and between his toes. Lameness and consequent irritation ensues, sometimes small bumps rising on his back. The seeds should be withdrawn and the puncture made swabbed over with antiseptic solution.

HARE-LIP
A congenital deformity, usually associated with Cleft Palate, already discussed. The lip has an open division making it impossible for the puppy to suckle effectively.

HARVESTERS (OR HARVEST MITES)
Small red creatures the colour of red pepper which abound the fields in summer. They cluster on the dog wherever they make contact and cause intense irritation. The best treatment is to dust him with 'Gammexane' powder as soon as he is back home.

HEAT STROKE
Often caused by thoughtless owners leaving their dog in a closed car during hot weather. A dog so mishandled should be limited to a drink of cold water to which a little salt has been added. His body should be bathed gently with cold water.

HERNIA
It is not uncommon for first-born puppies or those bred from a maiden, therefore inexperienced dam, to have a protuberant navel. This is caused by the agitated mother pulling on the umbilical cord, or by a dam whose extreme undershot jaw will disallow a clean bite of the cord close up to the whelp. Small bumps thus produced in the puppy's navel area are of little consequence and few would describe them as being unsound. However, puppies with large bumps are probably best left unpurchased, although veterinary treatment is invariably successful, but expensive.

There are other forms of hernia known as Inguinal Hernia (sometimes noted in a bitch's groin), the Scrotal Hernia and the Diaphragmatic Hernia. The last-named can be caused by an accident. All these are far more serious than the common Umbilical form referred to and need prompt surgical treatment.

HYDROPHOBIA (See Rabies.)

HYSTERIA
This mental disturbance, like the ordinary fit, although distressing to watch does not appear to worry the individual unduly, once the phase has passed. Worms, teething pains, etc. have been blamed for Hysteria. It is also engaged with the aftermath of Distemper. When it occurs the dog should be taken at once to a quiet, dark room, taking care to avoid being bitten. He should be left there until the fit has taken its course, making sure, of course, that nothing remains in the room with him which could cause him serious injury.

INCONTINENCE

Usually encountered in an elderly dog unable to hold himself for more than a few hours at a time without urinating. It is common too in a bitch, heavy in whelp with the puppies pressing on her bladder. Kidney troubles can show this as a symptom and advice should be sought at once in such cases. When dogs are seen to be incontinent due to any of the above causes, it is unkind to chastise them for their lapses. Put down newspapers or sand trays at night where they can urinate and not feel too guilty in doing so.

INTERVERTEBRAL DISCS

These are small bi-concave pads of fibro-cartilage which are inserted between adjoining vertebrae to allow flexibility and lessen concussion. These are thicker in some parts of the spine than in others, particularly in the joint between the dorsal and lumbar bones. They are thinnest between the dorsal bones themselves. Sometimes a dog suffers a slipped disc due to an accident or unexpected pressure. This is more likely in a longer backed specimen and the condition requires rest and careful manipulation.

LEANNESS

Some dogs seem never to furnish enough in body to complete correct balance with substance. A well-used stud dog is often such a problem to his owner, especially if the dog is wanted for exhibition too. The difficulty arises too with young males in the process of sexually adjusting themselves. Although not necessarily true, it is usually found that once the appetite can be promoted the dog will put on weight. Vitamin E Succinate is a useful encouragement and Wheat Germ Oil capsules will be found helpful. Appetites can be 'tickled' with tasty morsels such as cubes of Cheddar cheese, etc. but it is not suggested that the Staffordshire should be indulged beyond the realms of commonsense. Vitamin B can also be used to good effect when a dog needs more weight.

LICE

These tiny grey insects burrow under the dog's skin and cause him considerable irritation because he finds it impossible to dislodge them. The eggs can often be noted clinging to his coat and unless they are promptly removed and disposed of they will hatch out in less than a week and use him as their host. 'Gammexane' powder must be dusted liberally into his coat and a course of baths, using 'Seleen Suspension' will dispose of the lice and their eggs completely. The coat is sponged over thoroughly for at least ten minutes, but not rinsed. The dog should then be dried off.

MANGE

Like skin trouble in humans, the subject is only superficially understood, its forms appearing in such variety. Apart from the Eczemas and ordinary Dermatitis and Ringworm, covered individually in this chapter, the two kinds which concern most are Sarcoptic and Follicular (or Demodectic) Mange.

FOLLICULAR MANGE: This is caused by a mite which burrows into the follicles of the skin, causing the hair to fall out in small quantities at a time. The area so affected will become bare, red and raw and although at first the patches will appear on the cheeks, the skull and foreparts in sections not much larger than a 5p piece, they will eventually merge together substantially. A dog in an advanced state of the disease can be virtually denuded of coat. It will be found that the affected skin areas thicken perceptibly and look as though they have been dusted with a white ash or powder. The mites appear to emit a sort of poison which gradually debilitates the dog and can eventually prove fatal, for the victim becomes not only distressed with the irritation but seems to sink into a state of melancholia. On the other hand, if this pernicious mite is caught early in its attack it can be dispersed. There are a number of good proprietary remedies on the market and extra good feeding and exercise contributes to successful results. It is a disease which seems to attack the short-coated breeds more and care must be taken to ensure that all bedding used by a patient is destroyed and the kennel scrupulously cleaned out with strong disinfectant, for the mite can pass from one dog to another.

SARCOPTIC MANGE: This too is caused by a mite and causes intense irritation. It is usually noticed for the first time by what appears to be acne on the underbelly and inner thighs of the dog. On inspection it is clearly not acne but pustular spots as found in dry eczema, which break and encrust, forming scabs. Some hair loss is experienced and the skin becomes very dry. All kinds of remedies have been used including sulphur baths, polar bear's grease and various 'secret' recipes. Very often such afflictions beset a dog below par in health. As with other manges referred to, it is the first essential to condition the animal with nutritive food and exercise, givng him a sound and healthy internal groundwork for external treatment.

NEPHRITIS

Kidney inflammation, causing considerable pain, is sometimes caused by renal calculi, which are stones in the kidneys. In young dogs Leptospira canicola can infect through contact with the urine of dogs already infected. Loss of appetite, lumbar pains, thirst and vomiting, with coated tongue. A serious condition generally, and one likely never to be entirely dispersed.

NERVOUSNESS

This is a condition most undesirable in the Staffordshire Bull Terrier and viewed askance in any breed, for that matter. It can be due to close in-breeding, haphazard breeding or bad environment and ill-treatment. Sometimes it stems from puppyhood, when a dog is picked up suddenly and cruelly or the dog is left alone and hungry for extended periods. Bitches, for example, are sometimes forbidden the chance of a quiet and easy pregnancy. They should be kept away from annoyances and irritations until well after their puppies have been born. The best treatment for a nervous dog is reassurance by his owner. It can be soon discovered what brings an individual into a condition of fear and until he can face that situation again without a tremor, he should be conditioned, or trained to meet it. A good nerve tonic for dogs is Scullcap, from the plant Scutellaria, otherwise known as Helmet Flower. This forms an excellent herbal remedy.

OBESITY

A fat Stafford is an anathema. Quite apart from spoiling his general appearance, the extra weight around the loins militates against the athletic prowess expected of the breed and shortens his life. His food will have to be arranged on a strict diet, cutting out anything which is liable to fatten and concentrating almost entirely on raw meat. If these measures have no effect, the cause might be glandular, in which case the veterinary surgeon must be asked to diagnose.

POISONS

All cases of poisoning should be referred at once to the veterinary surgeon. First aid must be in the form of an emetic. This can be either a dessertspoonful of common salt in a quarter pint of water or a similar solution of mustard. A marble-sized piece of common soda will be effective too. If you know or suspect the cause of poisoning tell the veterinary surgeon when you telephone him. He will then be able to guide you in the treatment of the individual form.

POISONS (TYPES OF)

ALKALI: Probably occasioned by absorbing a domestic cleansing agent. Effective antidote is vinegar or lemon juice.

ARSENIC: Useful household remedy is to give dose of Epsom Salts.

ACID: First-aid. Give a knob of bicarbonate of soda.

COAL GAS: Remove unconscious dog to open air, prise open mouth, pull or extend tongue and apply artificial respiration. Keep dog quiet and warm while awaiting the veterinary surgeon.

COAL TAR (CARBOLIC): Phenol poisoning can come from a dog having walked over freshly tarred road, then licked his feet or one just washed using 'Lysol' or carbolic soap. Wash off offending matter, keep animal quiet, warm.

HYDROCYANIC ACID: Taken as a rule from eating laurel or wild cherry. Antidote: dextrose or corn syrup.

IODINE: Antidote: starch and water mixture, arrowroot, cornflour. Morphia and morphine derivatives can be given before and after the emetic.

LEAD: Taken from paint pigments. Antidotes: whites of eggs beaten in milk, milk of magnesia, Epsom salts (a dessertspoonful in about a quarter of pint of warm water), dilute sulphuric acid, or potassium iodide. High saline irrigation is important.

MERCURY: Taken as a rule by licking at skin ointments thereby absorbing bichloride of mercury, or coal-tar derivatives from mange lotions or rat poison. Antidote: whites of eggs beaten in milk or water (before and after the emetic), dilute sulphuric acid, gluten or wheat or potassium iodide.

PHOSPHORUS: Taken by puppies playing with and eating matches or by dogs eating baits set for rodents. Antidote: refrain from giving oily or fatty substances, even creamy milk, as these increase the solubility of the poison. Give three to five grains of copper sulphate or permanganate of potash every twenty minutes until the veterinary surgeon arrives. Epsom salts are effective too.

STRYCHNINE: The common medium of dog poisoners being very effective and rapid. Antidote: the best is an injection of apomorphia, others being chloral hydrate and amyl nitrate – these must be given by the veterinary surgeon. First aid entails an immediate emetic; try and give the patient butter, dripping and other fats. Keep in a dark room meanwhile.

Finally, it is as well to observe caution when giving laxatives. Many of these contain strychnine and an overdose of laxatives can prove fatal to a dog, especially smaller varieties. Violent purges notably those intended for humans are quite unsuitable for dogs. Any dogs so dosed and evincing symptoms of poisoning may require morphia or apomorphic hydrochloride injected subcutaneously.

RABIES

A disease commonly found in India and the East and not unusual in the Soviet Union. It is one of great antiquity, even being described by Aristotle in the fourth century BC. Epidemics of Rabies have been known and reported from Europe and in the early days England suffered similarly. The symptoms vary, but one indication is a marked change of manner and character of the dog, which becomes excited and is inclined to snap without reason. Sometimes the jaw drops and the hindquarters stiffen as though with paralysis. The cure for Hydrophobia appears unknown although protective vaccines have been developed which are highly recommended. Unfortunately, the disease now threatens Britain due to its encroachment from Europe. Animal smuggling contributes to the menace and Rabies is a notifiable disease.

RICKETS

This condition has been largely dispersed in dogs today due to the greater interest shown in them and better pre-natal care, and scientific rearing. A sufferer will have enlarged joints, with a tendency to walk almost on the hocks. The spine will be arched and the front bowed. Such a dog will never entirely cast off the condition, even with the best possible feeding and care, but he can be vastly improved upon by concentrating on highly nutritive foods such as raw, fresh beef, fresh eggs, milk and balanced calcium additives as soon as the condition has been diagnosed.

RINGWORM

A skin disease capable of being transferred to humans. The hair becomes thin and detached, making small round patches on the coat in typical ring shape. It is a fungoid disease and needs specialised veterinary treatment.

ROUNDWORM

Many dogs are infested with roundworm, but it is puppies who appear the main sufferers. The worm is easily dispersed these days, there being many proprietory medicines available to dog owners. In appearance the roundworm looks like vermicilli. It is creamy-pink in colour and about 4in to 5in long. Care has to be taken when dosing very young puppies and it is as well to let the veterinary surgeon arrange this unless the breeder is experienced and knows what he is doing. At one time it was necessary to starve a puppy prior to dosing, but modern methods do not require this. Usually one treatment will suffice, the worms being emitted orally and through the anus in coils. However, some breeders prefer to treat again when the puppies are about eight weeks old, the first attempt being a milder one at say five weeks of age. Once free from roundworm, the youngster will make rapid strides and thrive well.

TAPEWORM

An unpleasant parasite, its small segments adhering to the dog's anal region, revealing the infestation, which usually attacks adults rather than puppies. These segments look rather like grains of rice, but the worm itself can be many feet long inside the dog. It resembles a strip of creamy coloured tape or ribbon and causes great listlessness in its host. The dog's coat will be affected and he is likely to emit a pungent odour from body and breath. The Tapeworm is believed to be contracted either from the flea or by eating rabbit. The veterinary surgeon will know how to expel the worm quickly but treatment should be repeated twice yearly as reinfestation is likely.

Appendix

Staffordshire Bull Terrier breed clubs and their secretaries

Details change occasionally, so if you have difficulty in ascertaining the current officer you should contact the Kennel Club, 1 Clarges Street, London, W1 (01-493 6651) or the Kennel Club of the country concerned.

EAST ANGLIAN STAFFORDSHIRE BULL TERRIER CLUB: Mrs Joyce Shorrock, Weston Hall, Beccles, Suffolk. (Tel. Beccles 713472)

EAST MIDLANDS STAFFORDSHIRE BULL TERRIER CLUB: Mr J. Monks, 88 Briars Meads, Oadby, Leics. (Tel. Leicester 713122)

IRISH STAFFORDSHIRE BULL TERRIER ASSOCIATION: Mr G. O'Sullivan, 101 Farranferris Avenue, Farranree, Cork, Ireland.

IRISH STAFFORDSHIRE FANCIERS' CLUB: Mrs T. Cleary, 3 Granitefields, Dunlaoghaire, Co. Dublin.

MERSEYSIDE STAFFORDSHIRE BULL TERRIER CLUB: Mrs Marilyn Watson, 52 Radvers Drive, Orrell Park, Liverpool L9 8TD. (Tel. 051 525 1492)

NORTHERN COUNTIES STAFFORDSHIRE BULL TERRIER CLUB: Mrs Marlene Booth, 19 Westfield Avenue, Yeardon, Leeds, West Yorks. (Tel. 0532 504929)

NORTH EASTERN STAFFORDSHIRE BULL TERRIER CLUB: Mr T. Spashett, 118 Hambledon Road, Linthorpe, Middlesborough, Cleveland. (Tel. 0642 825176)

NORTHERN IRELAND STAFFORDSHIRE BULL TERRIER CLUB: Mr W. McKnight, 9 Mountcoole Gardens, Belfast, N.I. (Tel. Belfast 774204)

NORTH OF SCOTLAND STAFFORDSHIRE BULL TERRIER CLUB: Mrs J. Carmar, 97 Malcolm Road, Peterculter, Aberdeen, Scotland. (Tel. 0224 734441)

NORTH-WEST STAFFORDSHIRE BULL TERRIER CLUB: Mrs S. Dootsun, 45 Cecil Road, Eccles, Lancashire.

NOTTS AND DERBY DISTRICT STAFFORDSHIRE BULL TERRIER CLUB: Mr B. Grattridge, 3 Angela Avenue, Kirkby-in-Ashfield, Nottinghamshire. (Tel. Mansfield 752349)

POTTERIES STAFFORDSHIRE BULL TERRIER CLUB: Mr. L. Hemstock, 56 Cherry Avenue, Kirkby-in-Ashfield, Nottinghamshire. (Tel. Mansfield 753084)

SCOTTISH STAFFORDSHIRE BULL TERRIER CLUB: Mr A. W. Harkness, Senkrah Villa, Chapel Street, Carluke, Strathclyde. (Tel. 0555 70564)

SOUTHERN COUNTIES STAFFORDSHIRE BULL TERRIER SOCIETY: Mr A. Phillips, 37 Inglemere Road, Forest Hill, London SE23 2BE. (Tel. 01-699 0248)

SOUTHERN CROSS STAFFORDSHIRE BULL TERRIER CLUB: Mrs T. O. Smith, 145 Massey Street, Hastings, New Zealand.

STAFFORDSHIRE BULL TERRIER BREED COUNCIL OF GREAT BRITAIN AND NORTHERN IRELAND: Mr A. Mitchell, 6 Godolphin Way, Newquay, Cornwall. (Tel. 06373 6408)

STAFFORDSHIRE BULL TERRIER CLUB: Mr J. Beaufoy, 'Wayfarers', Yew Tree Lane, Bewdley, Worcestershire DY12 2PJ. (Tel. 0299 403382)

STAFFORDSHIRE BULL TERRIER CLUB OF CANADA: Mr I. Trott, 36 Cooksville Mews, 3175 Kirwin Avenue, Mississauga, Ontario, Canada.

STAFFORDSHIRE BULL TERRIER CLUB OF FINLAND: Mrs Irmeli Sauriom Kolmiranta, SF02820, Espoo 82, Finland. (Tel. 90-868 193)

STAFFORDSHIRE BULL TERRIER CLUB OF MASHONALAND: Mr V. Haines, 187 Glenside Drive, Strathaven, Salisbury, Zimbabwe.

STAFFORDSHIRE BULL TERRIER CLUB OF THE NETHERLANDS: Mr A. van Herpen, 'Melmars', Handem Huizen, 9200 Friesland, Netherlands.

STAFFORDSHIRE BULL TERRIER CLUB OF NEW SOUTH WALES: Mrs A. Bailey, P.O. Box 251, Seven Hills, NSW, Australia.

STAFFORDSHIRE BULL TERRIER CLUB OF SOUTH WALES: Mr S. A. Rumble, 85 Brynhyfryd Terrace, Ferndale, Rhondda, Mid-Glamorgan. (Tel. Ferndale 730141)

STAFFORDSHIRE BULL TERRIER CLUB OF THE TRANSVAAL: Mr R. Armstrong, 210 Barry Hertzog Avenue, Greenside, Johannesburg, South Africa.

STAFFORDSHIRE BULL TERRIER CLUB OF THE UNITED STATES, INC.: Rec. Secretary: Ms Barbara Gempler, 108 Farley Drive, Aptos, California 95003, USA. Corr. Secretary: Ms Karen Jacuzzi, 225 West Frier Drive, Phoenix, Arizona 85021, USA.

STAFFORDSHIRE BULL TERRIER CLUB, USA: Mrs Irma Rosenfield, 3215 N.56th Street, Omaha, Nebraska 68104, USA.

STAFFORDSHIRE BULL TERRIER CLUB OF WESTERN AUSTRALIA: Mrs J. Francis, 7 Solandra Way, Forrestfield 6058, Western Australia.

WESTERN STAFFORDSHIRE BULL TERRIER CLUB: Mrs Marian Fletcher, 9 School Road, Maesteg, Mid Glamorgan, South Wales. (Tel. 0656 733366)

Glossary of Terms

AFFIX: Affixes are usually attached to a dog's registered names in order to identify them with particular kennels. They should really be divided into Prefixes and Suffixes, the former to go before the dog's name (e.g. 'Bandits Bomber') the latter to be put after the name (e.g. 'Bella of Bandits').

ANGULATION: The angles formed where the bones meet at the joints. When applied to the hind limb it refers to the correct angle formed by the true line of the haunch bone, femur and tibia. In the forelegs it would refer to the line of shoulder bone, radius bone and humerus. Lack of angulation suggests straightness in these joints and such a condition could be reasonably considered an unsoundness.

A.O.V.: Any Other Variety. A show term used to indicate that class entries are invited from any other variety than the breed entered for in a previous class.

APPLE HEADED: With the skull rounded on top as in Toy Spaniels. A feature undesirable in the Staffordshire.

A.V.: Any Variety. A term used to indicate that entries are invited from any variety of breeds, including those entered from earlier classes. This applies to shows, stake classes and Field Trials.

B. or b.: Abbreviation for bitch, as described in dog show catalogues and on show entry forms.

BAD-DOER: A dog who thrives poorly, however well fed and cared for. Often, such a dog has never done well, even from birth.

BAD-SHOWER: A dog who cannot, or will not display himself properly and to advantage at shows. This can be due to boredom, obstinacy or nervousness.

BALANCE: Co-ordination of the muscles giving graceful action coupled with the overall conformation of the dog, the lateral dimensions of the dog should mould pleasingly with his vertical and horizontal dimensions. Equally, the head and tail should conform and contribute pleasingly to the balance of the dog's outline.

BARRELLED: A term pertaining to ribs which are strong and well rounded (like a barrel), allowing plenty of heart room.

B.B.: Abbreviation for Best of Breed.

BEEFY: Over-development of the hindquarters, which are thus rendered coarse.

BENCHED: Pertaining to a show where the dogs exhibited are relegated to benches.

BITCHY: An effeminate male.

BITE: Refers to the position of the upper and lower incisors when the dog's mouth is closed.

BLOCKY: Term used to describe the brachycephalic head, such as the Boston Terrier's. Also used to describe a short, stocky, cobby body such as the Bulldog's.

BLOOM: Glossiness or good sheen of coat, especially desirable on a Stafford.

BONE: A well-boned dog is one possessing limbs giving an appearance and feel of strength and spring without being coarse.

BR: Breeder, i.e. the owner of the dam of the puppies at the time of whelping.

BRACE: Two dogs of the same breed exhibited together.

BRINDLE: A mixture of dark and light hairs giving a generally dark effect, usually being lighter streaks or bars on a grey, tawny, brown or black background.

BRISKET: That part of the body in front of the chest and between the forelegs.

BROKEN COLOUR: Where the main coat colour is broken up by white or other hairs.

BROOD BITCH: A female kept solely for breeding purposes.

B.S. or B.I.S.: Best in Show or Best in Sex. A dog who has beaten all others or all others in this sex, respectively.

BURR: The irregular formation of the inner ear.

BUTTERFLY NOSE: When the nostrils are mottled or show flesh colour against the black pigment.

BUTTON EARS: Ears which drop over in front covering the inner cavity, as in the Fox Terrier.

CAT FEET: Short, round and 'tight' feet with compact, thick pads, the toes well muscled-up and arched.

C.C.: Challenge Certificate. A Kennel Club award signed by a judge for the best dog of his sex in breed at a Championship Show.

CH.: Champion. The holder of three C.Cs. awarded and signed by three different judges.

C.D.: Companion Dog. One holding this degree has passed a test for obedience and reliability.

C.D.(X).: Companion Dog (Excellent). A degree indicating that the holder has passed a severe test for obedience and reliability.

CHARACTER: A combination of the essential points of appearance and disposition contributing to the whole, and distinctive to the particular variety of dog to which the holder belongs.

CHEEKY: Exceptional development of the cheek muscles and cheek tissue.

CHOPS: The pendulous upper lips common to the Bulldog and certain Hounds, but faulty in the Staffordshire.

CLODDY: A low and very thick-set build.

CLOSE COUPLED: Short in back and loins.

COBBY: Of compact, neat and muscular formation. Like a cob horse.

CORKY: Compact, nimble in mind and body, lively and spirited.

COUPLING: That part of the body between the last ribs and the hip joints joined by the backbone.

COW-HOCKS: A dog is said to have cow-hocks when his hocks are bent inwards, thus throwing the hind feet outwards. A structural fault.

CREST: The upper part of the dog's neck.

CROPPING: The practice of trimming a dog's ears to make them small and to stand erect according to the requirements of his breed. This is forbidden in Britain and some American states, but common in Europe.

CROSS-BRED: The issue of parents of two different pedigree breeds.

CROUP: The area adjacent to the sacrum and immediately before the root or set-on of the tail.

CRYPTORCHID: The male dog whose testicles are abnormally retained in the abdominal cavity. Ineligible for show ring competition.

CUSHION: The fullness of the foreface obtained by the padding of the upper lips, in such breeds as the Bulldog and Mastiff.

D. or d.: The abbreviation for the Dog (Male) as described in dog show catalogues and/or entry forms.

DAM: The female parent of puppies. The term is generally used, but it has special reference to the bitch from the time she whelps the puppies to the time when she has finished weaning them.

DEW-CLAWS: Rudimentary fifth digits and claws found on the insides of the legs below the hocks.

DEWLAP: The loose pendulous skin under the throat. This is highly undesirable in the Staffordshire.

DISH-FACED: A concavity in the muzzle of the dog causing the nose to be tilted slightly higher than the stop.

DOME: Term which refers to the rounded skull in some dogs, such as the Spaniel.

DOWN-FACED: The opposite to dish-faced (q.v.) when the nose-tip is well below the level of the stop due to a downward inclination of the nose.

DOWN IN PASTERNS: Pasterns which being weak and sagging show an angle of the front feet forward and outward instead of the correct pastern (straight in line from the forearm to the ground).

DUDLEY NOSE: A wholly flesh- or coffee-coloured nostrils; quite distinct from the Butterfly Nose.

FANCIER: One who is interested in some phase of livestock breeding.

FILLED-UP: Usually refers to a dog's face with bulky cheek muscles.

FLANK: The dog's side between the last rib and hip.

FLEWS: The pendulous inner corners of the lips of the upper jaw.

FLY-EARS: Ears which are semi-erect and stand out from the side of the head.

FRONT: What can be seen of the front part of the dog except the head, having special reference to the soundness of brisket and forelegs.

GAIT: How a dog walks, trots or runs.

GAY TAIL: One which from root to tip is carried above the horizontal.

GOOD-DOER: A dog who thrives well without any special treatment. One who has done well from birth.

GOOSE-RUMP: A sloping croup, falling away too quickly with the tail set-on too low.

GRIZZLE: An iron grey coat colour, sometimes refers to a grey-brindle.

GUN-SHY: One who is frightened at the sight of a gun or its report.

HANDLER: A person who handles the exhibit in the ring at dog shows. More correctly refers to professional handler.

HARE-FEET: Feet which are rather long and narrow, like those of the hare. Undesirable in the Stafford.

HAW: The inner part of the lower eye-lid which is well developed, hanging down as in the Bloodhound. A fault in the Stafford.

HEAT: A bitch is said to be 'on heat' during her oestral period, when in 'season'.

HEIGHT: A dog's height is measured in a perpendicular line from the ground to the top of his shoulders (at the withers).

HOCKS: The joints in the hind legs between the pasterns and the stifles.

HUCKLE BONES: The top of the hip joints.

IN-BREEDING: The mating of closely-related dogs, done to perpetuate certain desirable characteristics, which exist already, at least to some extent.

INTERNATIONAL CHAMPION: A dog who has been awarded the title of Champion in more than one country. The term is not recognised officially by The Kennel Club.

LAYBACK: When the nose of the dog lies well back into the face as in some of the short-faced breeds such as the Bulldog.

LEATHER: The skin of the ear-flap.

LEGGY: So high on the leg that the dog appears unbalanced.

LEVEL MOUTH: When the jaws are so placed that the teeth meet about evenly, neither undershot, nor noticeably overshot.

LINE-BREEDING: The mating of dogs of similar strain, not too closely related.

LIPPY: When the lips overhang or are developed more than is correct.

LITTER: A family of puppies born to a bitch at one whelping.

LOADING: Refers to over-musculation or heaviness at the shoulders.

LOINS: That part of the body protecting the lower viscera and overlying the lumbar vertebrae between the last ribs and hindquarters. Fatness in the loin area is undesirable in the Stafford.

LONG-COUPLED: The opposite to close-coupled.

LUMBER: A dog having lumber is one with too much flesh, ungainly in appearance and clumsy in action. Not to be confused with the gawkiness of puppies.

MAIDEN: In the widest sense an un-mated bitch, but in exhibition parlance usually a dog or bitch not having won a first prize.

MASK: The dark markings on the muzzle of the Stafford, or the muzzle itself.

MATCH: A form of competition which is usually arranged privately between dog clubs. It is bound by the usual Kennel Club disciplinary rules.

MATRON: A brood bitch. One kept for breeding purposes.

MONORCHID: A male dog with only one testicle visible and descended into the scrotum. Such dogs are able to sire puppies, but are not considered so reliable as a dog which is entire, i.e. with both testicles descended into the scrotum. They are ineligible for show ring competition and may not be exported abroad unless the defect is made known to the prospective purchaser and accepted by him.

MUZZLE: The projecting part of the head combining the mouth and nose.

N.A.F.: Name Applied For.

N.F.C.: Not For Competition.

NOVICE: In the widest sense an inexperienced breeder or exhibitor, but in exhibition language a dog or bitch not having won two first prizes.

OCCIPUT: The bone at the top of the back of the skull which in some breeds is prominent as in most of the Hound group.

OESTRUM: The menstrual period. Known also as 'on' or 'in heat' or 'in season'. It lasts usually about twenty-one days, the bitch becoming ripe for mating between the tenth and fifteenth.

OUT AT ELBOWS: Having the elbow joints turned out from the body. A structural weakness.

OUT AT SHOULDERS: Having the shoulders outwards in a loose fashion so as to artificially increase the width of the dog's front. This is a fault in the Stafford.

OUTCROSS: The mating of unrelated dogs of the same breed but different strain.

OVERSHOT: Having the upper incisors projecting over and beyond the lower incisors.

PAD: The cushioned sole of the foot.

PARTI-COLOUR: A coat of two or more colours in patches; checkered or harlequin.

PASTERN: The lowest part of the leg below the knee on the foreleg or below the hock on the hindleg.

P.D.: Police Dog. A dog trained for police work.

PIG-JAW: A badly overshot jaw formation.

PREFIX: A kennel name which is usually put before a dog's registered name to identify it with that kennel. Not to be confused with the Suffix when the word follows a dog's name.

PRICK EARS: Ears which stand erect.

PUPPY: A dog under twelve months of age.

QUARTERINGS: The junctions of the limbs, referring especially to the hindquarters.

RACY: Slight in construction; rather long bodied giving an impression of speed rather than substance.

RANGY: Rather long in body, but with more substance than a racy dog.

RED: A general term for coat colours which range from fallow to chestnut, although more properly applied to the darker coats.

RED-SMUT: A term for a dog with a red or fawn coat usually with a dark face mask, dark spinal trace and black points. Red-smuts were common in Scotland at the turn of the century.

RESERVE: The fourth place after judging, for which a green prize card is awarded. It can refer to the runner-up in a class or a show.

RIBBED-UP: A compact dog with the ribs well barrelled.

ROACH-BACK: A back which arches upwards along the spine with particular emphasis over the loins, as in the Dandie Dinmont Terrier. A fault in the Stafford.

ROSE EARS: Ears which fold over exposing the inner burr.

SEASON: When a bitch menstruates she is said to be 'in season'. The oestral period.

SECOND MOUTH: A dog is said to have his 'second mouth' when his first, or puppy teeth are replaced by permanent teeth.

SECOND THIGHS: The muscular development of the leg between the stifle and the hock.

SELF-COLOUR: When a dog is one whole colour, some allowance being given for toning.

SEMI-ERECT EARS: Ears which are neither pricked nor falling forward. Such ears have usually the tips falling forward.

SEPTUM: The thin line which is seen to divide the nostrils.

SERVICE: A mating. The term given to the act of copulation when a bitch is served by a stud dog. When a fee has been paid and the service has proved unsuccessful, it is usual for the stud dog owner to allow a 'free service'.

SET-ON: The point where the tail is set on to the hindquarters.

SHELLY: Applying to the dog's body only which is narrow and shallow.

SIRE: The male parent of a dog or litter of puppies.

SNIPEY: When the dog's muzzle is weak, too long and narrow.

SOUNDNESS: The ability of a dog to do his job correctly, being sound physically, perfect structurally and in first-class mental health.

SPLAY FEET: Feet where the toes are spread wide apart.

SPRING: Refers to elasticity of rib, i.e. when the ribs are well rounded, sound and elastic.

SPREAD: Refers to the width of the front between the wide-spread forelegs of a breed such as the Bulldog. It can refer to the exaggerated front of any dog exhibited in an out-at-shoulders stance.

STANDARD: The official description of the ideal dog of the breed, as drawn up by a body of experts in that breed and used as a guide in judging.

STARING COAT: When a dog is out of condition his coat hair will be dry, unkempt and harsh. It will stand up and out from the skin. This is known as 'staring'.

STERN: The tail, normally restricted to sporting dogs.

STIFLE: The joint in the hind leg joining the first and second thighs and corresponding to the human knee.

STING: A tail which is fairly thin, even at the root or set-on.

STOP: The depression between and in front of the eyes.

STRAIGHT HOCKS: Hocks which are almost vertical, lacking resilience.

STRAIGHT SHOULDERS: Shoulders where the scapula and humerus join, forming an obtuse angle, being in almost a straight line and rendering the dog a poor mover.

SUFFIX: A suffix is the name of a kennel which is attached to the end of a dog's name in order to identify him with a particular kennel or breeder. Not to be confused with a prefix which is put before a dog's name.

SWAY BACK: A back which dips behind the shoulders because of poor local muscular development.

T.A.F.: Transfer Applied For.

THROATY: When the skin of the throat is too loose.

TICKED: When small marks of another colour appears on the main body colour. Applies usually to small dark black or brown marks on a white ground.

TIE: The term is used to describe the locking union of a mating pair.

TIGER BRINDLE: A mixture of light and dark hairs and stripes on a brindled or mottled ground.

TIMBER: A name of good bonal construction, especially used when referring to the forelegs.

TRACE: A dark, often diffused line running down the spine of some short-coated breeds. More evident during puppyhood it opens out and usually indicates colour richness with maturity.

TRANSFER: A change of ownership of a registered dog, duly reported, paid for and recorded.

TUCKED-UP: When the loins are lifted up as in the Whippet. When seen in a breed such as the Stafford, might indicate stomach pains, but should be investigated.

TULIP EARS: Ears which are carried erect, but curled to nearly resemble a tulip bloom. An old type of ear once common in the Old English Bulldog.

TURN-UP: The underjaw which turns up and out as in the Bulldog.

TYPE: The quality essential to a dog if he is to represent or approximate the ideal model of his breed based upon his breed Standard.

UNDERSHOT: Having the lower incisors projecting beyond the upper, as in the Boxer and Bulldog.

UNSOUNDNESS: Anything which impairs the usefulness of the Staffordshire, either of a temporary or permanent nature.

UPSWEEP: Synonymous with Turn-up.

VENT: Generally indicating the area surrounding the anus.

V.H.C.: Very Highly Commended. A show award fifth in order of placing. It carries no prize money.

WEEDY: Very lightly constructed, lacking substance.

WELL-SPRUNG: Well-formed in chest development and spring of rib.

WHEEL-BACK: An arched or convex back; as Roach Back.

WHELPS: Newly born puppies.

WHIP TAIL: A tail thick at the root, but tapering to a fine point.

WITHERS: The point where the neck joins the body in the region of the shoulders.

Index